THE QUILTING HOUSE

A HICKORY GROVE CHRISTMAS

ELIZABETH BROMKE

PROLOGUE

L iesel Hart stood behind a stretch of folding tables, each with a thick red tablecloth draped over it.

A honey-baked ham sat squarely in front of Liesel. Its rich glaze seeped into the slices she'd carved half an hour earlier, when the event had begun.

On either side of the ham, spread platters and dishes galore. Mashed potatoes and stuffing puffed like clouds in their serving bowls, most still half full.

A second share of cranberry sauce filled one of Liesel's own personal antique dishes—an heirloom from her mother. Creamed brussels sprouts waited inside a cast iron pan.

It was the Hickory Grove Community Christmas Dinner, and Liesel was overseeing everything from the recipes, to the decorations, down to the invitations. Although, there weren't exactly *invitations* to Little Flock's holiday supper. Both the Thanksgiving event and the Christmas event were open to the public with a particular emphasis on those who were in want of a place to spend their evening. A place with other people and with downhome food.

This particular year, Liesel had even coordinated a charitable raffle. Community members were generous enough to donate various goods and services, and Liesel would dole out raffle tickets with each plateful of food she passed along the serving line.

Among the batch of donations were gift certificates to The Beauty Shoppe, Maggie Engel's place of work; tickets to the Dotson Museum in Louisville, courtesy of Fern Monroe, curator; a whole selection of pies by Malley of local Malley's fame; a waterproof wristwatch from The Jewelers on Main; and other goodies, too.

Usually, one private individual from town would donate a healthy sum to cover all the costs of the food, paper products, and decorations. The priest would normally funnel this donation through Fern Monroe, who helped with the church's administrative duties from time to time, particularly when it came to financials and tithing. The Hickory Grove Charitable Committee would deem the individual the Secret Santa, an appropriate nickname, Liesel figured.

Liesel, herself, had offered up one of her handmade quilts. It was a project she had spent the year on, hoping she'd have a special person to whom to give the piece. This one, her mother had helped her with. It was a complicated pattern, and Liesel wanted it to be *just right*.

Ah, yes. Liesel's annual project. Each year, on New Year's Day, she made exactly one resolution. The thing of it was, however, that it wasn't so much a resolution as it was a *wish*. A private deal between Liesel and herself. A superstition, even.

Liesel would set about a big project. Maybe it was a crafting project—like a quilt. Or maybe it was a personal endeavor, like the year she committed to learning sign language. Her deal was this: if, by the time she was finished with her endeavor, she hadn't *met* someone yet, then that meant that she was working on the wrong thing.

If she *had* met someone by the time she'd accomplished her end goal for that year, then it meant she was headed in the *right* direction. And she had better see that endeavor through to the bitter end. This year, if she met someone by the time she'd finished her quilt, then she was meant to make quilts for the rest of her life. Just as her mother had before her. Afghans, quilts, and baby blankets. The house off of Main Street was chock full of them.

The idea behind this deal, you see, was that Liesel was at least doing something productive while she waited for Mr. Perfect.

Even now, being over the hill, a mustard seed of faith remained in her heart that she wasn't too old. She wasn't too *anything* to meet someone to love. Someone to love *her*, too.

"Merry Christmas," a gruff voice bellowed in front of Liesel as she studied the ham once again, willing it to carve itself.

She glanced up, her eyebrows pricking together.

The man standing before her was no charity case. He was a local. An employed, self-sufficient local. Lonesome maybe, but not in need of anything.

Liesel hadn't been confronted with this sort of thing quite yet. Mainly, she'd just served vagrants. Types who'd found themselves in Hickory Grove for a spell and needed a little boost, maybe. Never, however, had she served a perfectly capable, perfectly *healthy*, perfectly *handsome* man. It all felt a little biblical. Serving someone who didn't require service.

She flicked a glance left, then right, then left again. "Sorry?" she managed, her voice high pitched. Liesel cleared her throat and shook her head before forcing a smile. She didn't know this guy's circumstances. Having a job didn't mean everything. "Merry Christmas," Liesel added, her cheeks growing warm as she gestured to the ham. "I just need to shave off a fresh slice for you." She indicated the second half of the ham which she'd sliced only halfway.

His smiled broadened. "Here," he said, reaching for the knife laid alongside the platter. "Allow me."

Slowly, in measured, careful motion, he sawed into the meat, stopping here and there to assess his work. When he was done, he slid a thick slice onto his plate then passed it to Liesel.

She shook her head. "I'll eat after. With my mother. She's on her way." Liesel would hate to seem snooty. Then, as if she couldn't close her mouth once she'd opened it, she added, "She helped me with a project for the raffle, and so... she'll be here before then."

He gave a short nod, smiled again, and then replied, "Not sure I'll stick around for the raffle, but that's nice." She tore a ticket from her roll and passed it to him, but he protested. "Really, no sense in me getting a ticket."

Something in her motivated Liesel to push the ticket into his outstretched hand, her red-tipped fingers lingering a moment too long. "Take it, *please*," she urged.

He did, then thanked her and left.

And that was *that*.

Liesel didn't see where he'd gone to eat, as the place had started filling up just as soon as he'd left.

Later, though, once the raffle was underway and she was enjoying her own plate in private with her mother, he reappeared. Liesel tried to look elsewhere, but her mother, being a, well, *mother*, stared at him a moment too long. Liesel was certain that her mother's stare was the reason he then joined them at the far edge of one of the tables, where Fern would soon begin the raffle.

"Dinner was delicious," he said, lowering into the open seat beside her.

Liesel forced her focus to her plate and replied mildly, "Thanks. I didn't cook it all. Had lots of help. Hickory Grove really knows how to come together." She tried to stave off the ice in her tone, withholding the implication that this guy was a hanger-on. A moocher. A well-employed, well-built, attractive *moocher*. The worst kind.

But he nodded dismissively. "I'm excited for the raffle." Then his voice dropped. "You convinced me to stick around."

"Oh?" Liesel was growing edgier by the moment.

"Sure. Got my eye on a few things."

Liesel lifted an eyebrow and shoveled the last of her potatoes into her mouth, wiping it with a napkin then taking her empty plate and her mother's to a nearby trash can.

She tried to shrug off the nagging feeling she had that there was something *missing* about the evening. And once *he'd* joined her at the table, it roared to life like a sign of some sort. A sign her intuition couldn't quite read. Or maybe a sign that her intuition was all off.

Fern came over and helped her manage the raffle. First went the gift certificates—the most prized possessions, by and large. Then a camping set. The watch with a programmable GPS—the only thing a jeweler could think of to give that might actually be useful. Then, some other practical items. Finally, Liesel's quilt came up. The last item to be raffled. At other types of events, all those who'd won something or who hadn't put in for the raffle would have left by now. But at the Hickory Grove Community Christmas Dinner, every last attendee remained until the bitter end.

Even *him*.

Liesel held the quilt open. The pattern had been her mother's idea: the eight-pointed star. Only one, nearly imperceptible error existed in the quilt, as was tradition (Liesel was a good quilter, and her mother was a great one, but it was only God who never erred). The red and white fabric, varieties of floral print, added an extra element of the yuletide season. Making this particular quilt had taken far longer than Liesel had expected. Yes, she knew it was a difficult pattern, but her goal was near perfection, and even *near* perfection took time. Even with the guidance of her mother, a master quilt-maker. When they at last finished it, Liesel said a private prayer, the quilt across her lap, reminding God of her deal. If she didn't meet someone by that Christmas dinner, when she gave away the fruit of her labors, then she'd find her next project.

Indeed, the attendees all reacted appropriately as Fern explained on Liesel's behalf the pattern and that Liesel handmade the whole of it alongside her mother.

Mamaw Hart, as the grandkids had taken to calling her, was a pistol of a woman, and a sweetheart to boot. And she was proud of Liesel. Of the quilt they'd made together *and* of Liesel. Adopted or not, Mamaw had been a good mother. A great one, even. Was she enough to stave off the tug in Liesel's heart? The tug that she was missing *something*. Or, perhaps, *someone*. Maybe not, but then... Liesel didn't blame her, surely. She didn't blame anyone for the circumstances of her own birth and, later, adoption. She accepted it. She accepted and tried to find ways to fulfill herself in the aftermath of that early, unrememberable incident in her own life.

Fern dug her hand into the raffle ticket jar—a glass fish-bowl Liesel had decked in red and green ribbon.

Liesel looked at the man sitting just near her. She still couldn't pin him down. Why was he *there*?

Just before Fern withdrew the winning ticket, he winked at Liesel. She felt herself flush deep red and quickly glanced away from him, unmoored by the lascivious gesture. Even so, her pulse raced, and her heart throbbed in her chest, and she was entirely incapable of quelling either sensation.

Liesel tried to ignore him.

But then, once Fern had read the numbers aloud twice, her smooth-as-butter Louisville drawl lifting like a carol across the room, the man shot up from his seat. He then joined Liesel and Fern at the head of their table, clapping along with the whistling, cheering crowd.

Fern smiled to him, congratulated him, and passed the quilt his way.

Then, in a moment of absolute *indecency*, the man leaned into Liesel. "I'll cherish this," he whispered, smiling genuinely as he took the quilt, then waved to Fern and the crowd.

As he stood near her, she smelled Christmas on him. Nutmeg aftershave or cinnamon hair gel—who knew? But it was heavenly, and it was all Liesel could do to give a brief nod of her head, a smile, and then turn to Fern. "I've got to go."

Her face burned bright, but still, her hand made its way to the spot on her cheek where his lips nearly brushed her skin. A stranger's lips. Someone familiar's lips. It was all the same. Wasn't it?

By the time she composed herself in the kitchen and was ready to re-emerge and accost him—accuse him and chastise him and drink in his scent and his kindness all over again, Fern appeared in the door.

"Shame, he had to go," she murmured casually. "Great guy."

Liesel simply nodded. Then, she frowned. "I don't mean to pass judgment," she began in earnest, "but do you know why he came by? He doesn't seem—"

Fern blinked before a chuckle erupted from her lips. "He was Secret Santa this year."

Surprise filled Liesel's chest, but still she couldn't push away the brashness of the experience. The discomfort. The distinct impression that the quilt—tedious blocks of that precious, intricate eight-pointed star, designed to guide its owner to the light—wasn't meant for him. It was probably meant for *her* all along.

She should have kept it. Donated something else, like fifty bucks or a ticket to the zoo. And kept the quilt.

Now certain she'd never see the piece again, Liesel realized this was it. Her deal had come to fruition. She hadn't *met* anyone by now, and the quilt was done and gone—a piece of her and a piece of her mother to some middle-aged jock with a little extra cash and a random will to pitch in at Little Flock for once in his life.

Liesel let out a sigh and smoothed her red sweater dress. She'd have to find a new project.

This time, it wouldn't be a quilt.

STEP 1: BEFORE YOU BEGIN

"**M**ama," little Liesel whined, falling into her seat at the kitchen table like a rag doll. "I'm too cold to do anything." This was the honest truth. Snow packed against the house, challenging the Hart family's potbelly stove.

Christmas was a month out, but their southern corner of Indiana had an early cold snap. A wee early cold snap. Piles of snow were perfect for younger children desperate for a good sledding, but Liesel was a bit older now. Colder, too.

"Here, now, doing something will warm you up," her mother chided. "Sit up straight, Liesel."

Liesel did as she was told, and her mother went on.

"See, now, I'm starting a new pattern, and it's the perfect time. You said you wanted to make a quilt. Pay attention, girl."

Liesel did want to make a quilt. And it was true that doing something would warm her up. She knew this well enough from her part-time job cleaning the parish hall. Snowed in as they were, though, there were only two options in the Hart home: scrub the toilets or listen to her mother's quilting seminar. The *latter was easily preferable. Liesel shifted her attitude accordingly.*

On the table, where they'd normally have supper and read the Bible, her mother had laid out tidy stacks of materials and tools—all familiar to Liesel since it seemed that Mama Hart was always quilting. But unfamiliar, too. Liesel had been interested since she was knee-high to a grasshopper but never interested enough to sit still and watch on as her mother instructed her.

Now, though, she was old enough, and that had to count for somethin'.

"Firstly," her mother went on, "you take stock of what you've got. No sense in wasting good fabric or supplies by running out to the crafting store and spending money you ain't got."

"What crafting store?" Liesel asked. This piqued her curiosity. If there was a crafting store, she might like to go there and browse, probably.

"Out in Louisville," her mother answered patiently. "The Crafting House somethin' or other." She sighed. "Anyhow, you take your stock, see?" The woman pressed a small index finger, the nail bare and blunt and the knuckle crooked despite her relative youth. "The most important thing is the fabric. Now, if we were making a scrap quilt, maybe an antique crazy or the like, well, we'd have more options in fabric."

"What kind are we making?" Liesel interjected, leaning forward as she inspected a tower of folded material—half of it crimson red and patterned and the other half cream colored and plain.

"Shoo-fly. It's best to learn on a shoo-fly pattern," her mother answered. "Bein' as I have last year's Christmas discount cotton, that'll be just fine. And seein' as we have a month, may as well push to make it in time."

"A month?" Liesel frowned. "You never finish a quilt in a month."

"This year I will, because I'll have you. And anyway, we'll keep it small."

"Who's it for?" Liesel asked. Her mother made quilts for baby showers and weddings and this, that, and the other.

"It's for Little Flock. They can do with it what they please, but it's always best to keep charity at the forefront of your mind when it comes to quiltin'."

This was a classic Mama Hart-ism. She was service-oriented and charity-driven. Ever since Liesel could remember, they were volunteering for this or showing up to help with that.

Liesel wasn't too sure about giving away the first ever quilt she'd make, but then if that was her stance, she probably didn't have charity at the forefront of her mind. And therefore, she'd be breaking the first rule of quiltin'.

"You have a lot of leftover material," Liesel pointed out, her eyes shifting to a secondary stack.

"I buy off-season. If you have a passion for something, Liesel, you do whatever you have to do."

"So, what's next?" Liesel asked, studying the third stack of fabric—white cotton, more supple than the other two stacks. Batting, Liesel knew. Beyond all the fabric were the other tools her mother commonly had out when she was quilting. Shears, rotary cutter, cardboard, needles, her pin cushion, prickly like a little cactus, and spools of thread. The thread she'd laid out for the day was a near match to the cream-colored cotton fabric. "Do we have to prewash and iron?" Liesel asked.

Her mother smiled. "I don't need to prewash this. It's nice to have the fabric stiff to begin."

"Where's your sewing machine?" Liesel glanced around, befuddled at its absence. An old Singer passed down from Liesel's grandmother.

"We're not there yet. Not by a ways," her mother smiled and

drew the back of her finger down Liesel's cheek. "Your patience will be key with quilting, Liesel."

Liesel took a deep breath. "I don't have much patience," she complained, rubbing her hands up and down her arms to generate a bit of warmth. "Can we just make some hot cocoa or somethin'?"

The woman propped her hands on her hips. "Everyone has patience. Deep down." She collected Liesel's hair and plaited it loosely. "This is coming from the most impatient woman of all. Trust me when I say that waiting for somethin' increases that somethin's value. Always."

"If I'm patient, I'll make a nicer quilt, I get it."

"Patience applies to much more in life than quilting, sweet girl." Her mother finished the plait and lowered down next to Liesel. "I promise."

"All right then." Liesel cinched the braid her mother had made into a tie from her wrist. "The shoo-fly quilt. Like the pie, then. Is that what the blocks will look like when it's done? A pie? Or a fly..." She frowned, and her mother laughed.

"Another name for this pattern is the Hole in the Barn Door. We'll cut triangles and squares and position them into something like this." Her mother twisted to a box of scrap fabric and pulled out several pieces, folding and smoothing them into a pretty display on the table in front of Liesel. "See?"

"Hole in the Barn Door," Liesel said dreamily, mesmerized by the pattern. A square sat prominently in the center. The top tip of a triangle kissed each corner of the square, abutted against a second triangle that matched those squares along the sides of the center square. Liesel didn't quite see why it was called shoo-fly or hole in the barn door or anything.

"I don't see it," Liesel said, cocking her head and peering hard to see an image that wasn't there.

"Well that's the second rule of quilting," her mother answered, sharing Liesel's gaze. "It's part patience, you see, and part artistry."

"And," Liesel added pointedly, "part magic."

CHAPTER 1—GRETCHEN

Gretchen Engel looked up from her sewing machine, an antique Singer she'd stationed by the window of the loft in her family's barn. A year earlier, she'd claimed the space as her own makeshift apartment and crafting studio.

Snow fell outside. Oversized, fluffy flakes of the stuff, surreal looking.

Inches of white already blanketed the wooded forest beyond her window, padding the barn from outside noise. That of her family, who lived in the house next to the barn.

Christmas music, tinny and somber, drifted from her CD player—yes, CD player. The one her mother had found at a yard sale the summer before. Gretchen didn't mind being behind the times when it came to technology, though. She liked the comfort of a commercial-free listening experience, even if "Little Drummer Boy" skipped on the chorus.

She returned her attention to the sewing machine, threading the bobbin with red, silken thread, and replacing the metal plate.

Then, Gretchen reached for the white fabric, cut in the

shape of a stocking and pinned inside out in preparation to be sewn up. She adjusted everything just so, lowered the foot, and set about running the would-be Christmas gift through, slowly, then quickly. Smoothly, the gentle whir lulling her into a trance.

After finishing the length of the stocking foot and turning up carefully to head back toward the top of it, Gretchen let out a sigh of relief.

This was the first one that hadn't tangled the thread and snagged everything up.

Her shoulders relaxed, she pulled the fabric out the back far enough to snip the thread and admire her work.

Simple and clean, if a little bland. She'd doll the piece up, adding applique reindeer to the cuff, once she'd sewn that part by hand and added looping stitches around the whole of it—for a charming effect. For now, though, it was good progress. She was due at the Inn in half an hour, and she still needed to get ready.

Gretchen drew the cloth cover over her machine, piled her fabric neatly to the side of her sewing table, and descended the ladder into the bottom level of her barn house.

In the previous year, she'd managed to make the space cozy and homey, adding rustic touches from trips to various yard sales and estate sales around Hickory Grove and in neighboring areas.

It wasn't until her boyfriend broke up with her, however, that Gretchen had really settled in. Clinging to the belief that Theo Linden would eventually whisk her away to a shiny new apartment near Notre Dame, where he was on scholarship, proved to be little more than a pipe dream. Plainly put, the two were far too opposite to *work*. Gretchen was a beauty-school dropout who worked part-time at a diner and part-time at a bed-and-breakfast. She had three much-younger siblings to babysit and a mom with a new husband and an in-home business—hair, of course.

Theo, on the other hand, was the only child of local sweetheart, Miss Becky Linden Durbin, who owned and ran a bookshop in town. Theo was up north, studying law, just like his stepfather before him, in one of the best private universities in America and on a full-ride academic scholarship, to boot.

See? Opposites. Total opposites. And although opposites may attract... that didn't necessarily mean their strength didn't eventually putter away.

But the silver lining to the end of that relationship was Gretchen's newfound joy in making the barn behind her family's farm a true home. Any extra time she had, she worked on it, sanding bare wood, staining or painting it, and filling the hollow and vast space with the perfect pieces to suggest she was much, much more than a beauty-school dropout with two part-time jobs.

One day, Gretchen promised herself, she really *would* be more than that. She would, like her mother, own her own business, right there in that barn. And whether she had a smart boyfriend with a fancy college degree or a downhome boy with scuffed work boots and a rusty pick-up truck, well, that just wouldn't matter.

Because Gretchen would have her *own* thing going.

A crafting business, ideally.

Just as she tugged her down coat on and slung her handbag over her shoulder, her phone chimed. Gretchen snatched it from the arm of the sofa and made her way outside, where the snow had taken a break, but the sky was heavier yet—dark and wet and frigid.

She glanced at the screen. A text message awaited her. One line. Simple. Timely. And aggravatingly cute.

"I'll be home for Christmas..."

Gretchen did a doubletake of the sender's name, surprised and yet *unsurprised* to confirm that, yes. It was Theo.

Only in your dreams, she thought and shoved the device deep into her pocket.

CHAPTER 2—LIESEL

Liesel stomped her feet on the front mat at the Hickory Grove Inn, where her nephew and his wife lived and worked.

Liesel's nephew, Luke, was at Hickory Grove High School, running the final pre-season track workout before the holidays. He was the sort of coach who could get away with hosting weight training sessions two days from Christmas.

But that's what made him good. That and his colleague, Mark Ketchum. Hickory Grove transplant and immediate town favorite. His easy manner and broken history—losing a wife years earlier—had endeared him to the locals. Not Liesel, though. She was a hard sell on coach types. Unless the man was her nephew, in which case, she made an exception.

Liesel rang the bell at the front desk, a habit more than a courtesy, as she shook all thoughts about the sweet man who'd ushered her down the aisle the summer before. Not *her* aisle, mind you. *Luke's* aisle. Luke and his wife, Greta.

"Aunt Liesel," Greta greeted her with a bouncing baby on her hip. Tabby, the apple of her parents' eye.

Liesel sort of hated that Greta called her aunt. It felt... contrived. Still, she was the picture of sweetness, Greta. She and her little baby girl, each bundled in snow-white sweaters, black leggings, and red knit beanies—a gift from Liesel ahead of what was turning out to be a cold and wet winter. That they matched so impeccably might have annoyed Liesel too, but they wouldn't be matching if she hadn't knit them matching winter hats, probably. It was Liesel's own fault, then. Still, she couldn't suppress a smile as she let Tabby curl her chubby little baby finger around Liesel's. It drove a pang to the middle-aged woman's heart. The sort of pang that a woman in her circumstances could do little to temper. More volunteering at the hospital nursery. A rejuvenation in attitude toward her Sunday school classes. Yes. Those would have to do to fill the longing Liesel couldn't seem to shake every time she laid eyes on darling Tabby.

"Greta, hello." Liesel greeted the young mother with a kiss on the cheek after duly tending to Tabby's attention. "How've you been?" Liesel was stopping by on her way to the airport. She had long ago planned a holiday trip to Birch Harbor, Michigan, where she had some business needing attending. Family business, sort of. Maybe something more.

"Great. Cold, but great. We're doing our grocery shopping later today—that is if the weather holds out. Maybe you'd like to join me?" Greta's eyes danced desperately. Liesel felt sorry for the girl. Greta had yet to make ins with the local housewives and mothers. It could be hard for an outsider in Hickory Grove, especially one of the female persuasion. Sometimes too hard. Maybe that was why even Liesel had been shopping for a new life. To shake loose the small-town claws that had long ago sunk into her skin, pulling her back instead of pushing her forward in life.

Then again, she couldn't blame Hickory Grove for her own shortfalls. Anything Liesel lacked had entirely to do with something engraved much deeper down. Even deeper than one's hometown.

"Oh, no," Liesel replied. "I'm here and gone. Just wanted to deliver gifts, since I'm not staying in town this year." She narrowed her gaze at her niece-in-law, awaiting a fuss to be made over Liesel's controversial choice to *leave town* for the holidays. Liesel could hear it now, across church pews at Little Flock and in line at the corner market: *Did you hear? Liesel Hart isn't in town for Christmas!* Such drama.

Greta blinked. The baby fussed in her arms.

"Tabby, sh. Shh," the young mother cooed. "Oh, Aunt Liesel, I thought you weren't going until *after* Christmas. This is just terrible news." She frowned and shook her head.

Liesel smiled. "That's kind of you to say, but I have family there. Family I haven't... I haven't spent much time with, you see." Liesel was thoughtful on the matter. She gestured over her shoulder. "Will you hold the door for me while I shuttle everything inside?"

Greta pressed her mouth into a line, Baby Tabby gurgling contentedly. "Oh, it's biting cold outside. Here, let me help. I'll just put her in her bouncer and be right there."

Liesel went out ahead of Greta, careful on the sidewalk. Salt had melted the ice well enough, but with a schedule to keep, it wouldn't do for Liesel to be reckless.

She walked toe-heel down the path, mentally playing out her plans. First, the drive to Louisville. Then the flight. From there, a car service would collect her. They'd drive down to Birch Harbor, where she'd stay for an entire week at the Heirloom Inn. She'd reconnect with relatives she'd never known. She'd research her parentage. Learn more about from whom she'd come and why.

Her flight wasn't for a few hours, but still she planned to arrive at the airport as early as possible, to be safe. After all, what with the looming storm, the sky was dark and roads treacherous. She'd have to drive slowly.

As she arrived back at her car and opened the hatch, she caught a glimpse of the figure of a younger woman walking down from behind the property, where the parking lot was situated, and toward the front of the Inn.

Liesel knew it was Gretchen Engel, Maggie Devereux's sweet-natured bookworm. Gretchen was the sort of small-town girl who everyone knew and no one knew. Liesel had seen her everywhere, from waiting tables at Malley's, to doing odd jobs for the seamstress up by Hickory Grove High, and down here, at the Inn. For being so ubiquitous, however, Gretchen kept to herself, just as she did now. Her head ducked low under a chunky knit cap, her hands tucked deeply into the pockets of her down jacket. An oversized boho bag hung along her side. Boots to her knees. She half-jogged along the slick walk and ducked inside, nearly colliding with Greta, with whom she exchanged a few brief words before the latter closed the door.

"Okay!" Greta arrived next to Liesel and chirped through the frigid air, her breath visible in white puffs. "Gre*tchen* just got here, so she'll take over with Tabby. Let me help you, Aunt Liesel." Greta always overemphasized the second syllable in Gretchen. A way to help distinguish the two with uniquely similar names but one of those off-putting things about her. Probably one of the things that turned some locals against her, too. Liesel felt for Greta. She tried hard. Really, she did.

Liesel forced a smile. Maybe it was the travel anxiety

putting her so on edge. Or the weather. Too cold for before Christmas. Usually, Hickory Grove didn't see harsh winters at all. And when it did, it was January or February by then. She hauled a cardboard box from the back of her car, neatly wrapped packages snugly organized inside like a game of Tetris.

Liesel didn't actually know that reference. Luke had used it when they were moving him into the house behind the Inn. He considered himself a "Tetris master" due to his ability to perfectly organize furniture, boxes, and everything else into the hollow chamber of a moving trailer. She'd shelved the reference for her own future use. It was Liesel's way of trying to preserve her own edge. Her modernity. This was becoming harder and harder, though. To keep up with it all—all the social media apps, all the apps *period*- Liesel couldn't do it. So, when she did learn a new term or phrase, she shelved it.

Liesel was fashionable and nice looking *enough* and everything that a woman of a certain age needed to be to earn some modicum of respect. Still, those little truths didn't stop the gray hairs. Nor did they reverse the past and change the fact that while Liesel stayed up on her manicures and hair appointments, and while she ate well and exercised, she could never retrace her steps. She could never be the young temptress that Greta, for example, surely was. She would never garner the attention of a young male. Or even an old one. She'd never known a man's romantic love nor would she likely get that experience now.

It was simply too late.

Anyway, Liesel had *more* important things. Like figuring out how in the world she was going to make it to the airport with the increasingly blustery wind and a fresh round of fat, whirling snowflakes.

Greta's flouncy blonde hair blasted back from her face, and her pinkish lips turned purple. "Let's get this inside!" she called through the loudness swirling around them as she took the box. "This is crazy!" she cried.

Liesel grabbed the second box, managed to will her hatch shut with her elbow then followed the girl inside to where Gretchen was bouncing Tabby on her hip like a little mother.

"Whew," Greta remarked, carrying the box through to the parlor where her Christmas tree stood in all its glory.

The lights flickered on and off. Liesel's stomach clenched as she looked around. "What was that?"

"Power," Greta answered mildly. "It did that a little while ago. The snow is so heavy on those lines."

A chill coursed through Liesel, though she couldn't tell if it was her stress or the cold. She heard the furnace kick on and relaxed. "Do you all have a back-up generator here?" She worried about Greta and Luke. They sometimes seemed ill-prepared to be so... on their own. Even though her nephew was self-sufficient and strong, that didn't always translate to grown-up stuff. Certainly not to being head of a family. She worried about this quite a lot.

Greta blinked. "No. But we've got the fireplace, of course. And loads of candles. Generators are expensive," she added, as if to reassure Liesel that she knew what she was doing, just couldn't afford any frills. Greta was sensible that way, and Liesel did appreciate this. When she'd lived for a season at Saint Meinrad's, she, herself, had come to appreciate the simple life. They had no generator, either. If the power went out in summer, you opened the windows. In winter? You stoked a fire.

Surely, Luke had stocked plenty of wood.

And anyway, if Greta's décor was any indication, the

little Hart clan and their Inn were well prepared for the winter. Beautiful Christmas decorations filled the foyer and the parlor.

For scrimping by on her husband's teacher's salary and an innkeeper's wage, Greta knew how to make the most of the holidays. They'd cut their own fresh tree from the forest, Liesel knew. Greta had made the garland herself—painstakingly stringing popcorn down lines of thread and singling out individual strands of dollar-store tinsel until the whole of the tree glowed puffy white and shimmery.

Liesel followed her and set the second box down, and Gretchen and Tabby followed Liesel.

"Hi Gretchen," Liesel greeted, managing to strike a cheery tone despite her growing nerves.

"Hi, Miss Liesel," Gretchen replied kindly. "How've you been?"

"Good, real good." Liesel smiled at her then lowered and helped Greta unpack the boxes and arrange the packages beneath the bottom boughs.

"My, Aunt Liesel," Greta went on, "You're spoiling us!"

Liesel waved her off, pushing up from the floor and smoothing her overcoat, wishing she'd shed it at the door; it was stiff and heavy and too formal. No doubt it'd be awkward to carry onto the plane, and then what? She wouldn't stow it beneath her seat and get it dirty. She'd have to keep it on her lap and—oh! The pain of traveling!

"Are you staying for Christmas, Miss Liesel?" Gretchen asked, handing Tabby off to her mother.

Liesel shook her head. "I've got a flight out to Michigan. Visiting, um, *family*, I suppose you could say."

"In this weather?" Gretchen asked, glancing through the window. It had been snowing off and on all day, but the wind had only just picked up. And boy, had it, too.

Liesel followed Gretchen's gaze. "Well, I haven't gotten a notification of any cancellation."

"Here," Greta pulled her phone out, tapping away masterfully as Liesel pursed her lips and crimped her brow. "I'll check. What airline?"

Liesel frowned deeper. "Oh, right. Um—TransAir. Flight 4820."

Greta flashed her phone Liesel's way. "Oh, dear, Aunt Liesel. Look."

Liesel didn't know what she was looking at, and her helplessness was evident, because Gretchen then leaned in to see the screen, interpreting the information right away. She pointed to fine print below the flight number and airline. "Grounded."

"But that's okay, Aunt Liesel," Greta cheered, "you can stay here for Christmas after all!"

CHAPTER 3—GRETCHEN

Gretchen did not know Liesel Hart very well. The woman was a Hickory Grove native, yes. And she was ultra-involved at Little Flock Catholic, sure. But seeing as Gretchen was a bit of a loner, the woman's local prestige didn't mean much to the twenty-year-old.

As for Christmas plans, *where* the icy woman celebrated was of little never mind to Gretchen, anyway. She already had her own plans. The usual Engel family Christmas. This year, as the one before, they'd be celebrating at the farm. Rhett would be there. Her father would also make an awkward appearance, no doubt. With any luck, no argument would break out and things would be more than civil. Maybe even merry.

Then, that evening, she'd report back to the Inn to cover a night shift for Greta.

This was all taking place in just two days' time, and Gretchen was anything but ready. Fortunately, she'd thought to stow a small sewing project in her handbag for downtime at the Inn. But all she could afford to do this year was finish up stockings—one for each person in her life—

and add a few small gifts. Truth be told, Gretchen did have enough money to do something more elaborate... but that was only if she dipped into her meticulously maintained savings account.

In fact, this was a point of internal conflict for her: to splurge on family and spoil them rotten? Or to stay the course with saving up for her business plan?

With mere hours, basically, until Christmas, she was running out of shopping time anyway.

Thank *goodness* it was just the family Christmas she had to worry about. No big to-do at Theo's mom's house to worry about. No Friendsmas, as was becoming a silly trend. Just her mom, the two dad-figures in her life, two brothers, and one sister. It was more than she could handle, really.

Theo's text nagged the back of her mind. But she was strong enough to ignore him. Gretchen refused to become a hometown holiday girlfriend. That's what she called the girls who didn't get as far as their boyfriends and who waited in the wings for the boys to return home for Christmas and Easter and the Fourth of July. No, when Gretchen broke up with Theo, it was *for good*.

Tabby started fussing, and Gretchen made a mental note to finish the booties she'd started crocheting for the baby's gift, undermining the whole point of keeping her Christmas small this year.

And *that* reminded her that she'd really better get something for Greta, too. Maybe even Luke. They were her employers, after all.

But if she got something for Greta and Luke, would she need to get something for her shift manager at Malley's? Should she put together a wreath and lay it across Malley's grave, too? Yes, she really should.

The anxiety about gift-giving was getting to Gretchen. Really, it was.

Greta moved the baby up to her shoulder and patted her back vigorously. "Aunt Liesel," she said, "I wouldn't even drive *home* if I were you. Not in this."

All three women neared the window and looked outside. Snow whipped in white cyclones beyond. It was borderline blizzard conditions.

"I've never seen anything like this," Gretchen murmured.

"We had this when I worked upstate. It's a whiteout." Greta rocked Tabby. "I'm sorry, Aunt Liesel, but it looks like you're stuck here. At least for a little while. Maybe it's a microburst, or whatever they're called. They usually sweep in and out in no time."

Hopefully, Greta was right—that the storm would be on its way faster than Frosty could melt. Gretchen didn't want to be the bearer of bad news... but they had no vacancies in the Inn. Of course, she *herself* was used to staying awake through the night, keeping busy with a book or a craft. Would Greta let Liesel sleep on the sofa in the parlor? Would she stay awake through the night, too? Sitting by the window, willing away the snow so she could get the heck out of Hickory Grove?

Sounded miserable to Gretchen.

"Surely the weather's not that bad," Liesel protested, tapping her red-painted nails against her lips.

Greta and Gretchen shared a worrisome glance.

"Miss Liesel, it does look bad out there. And if your flight is cancelled, anyway—"

Liesel snapped her fingers. "I need to call Michigan."

"Call Michigan?" Greta asked.

"Mm," Liesel answered. "Let them know about the flight. Maybe it's just delayed. Or maybe there's another way."

"Another way?" Greta asked. She was beginning to sound like a record player, stuck. "Oh, no, Aunt Liesel. You're staying in Hickory Grove tonight. *Here*, in fact. I'm nervous about so much as walking over to the house," Greta added fearfully as she swayed left and right with Tabby, who'd fallen asleep, drunk in her mother's cuddle.

"I think you're overreacting," Liesel murmured. "Let me call my contact in Michigan, and we'll go from there." She lifted her hand to the window. "It only just got bad. I bet it doesn't last."

Liesel left the room, moving into the kitchen as Greta and Gretchen and Tabby remained, staring out through the window, enchanted by the snowstorm. It looked very lasting, in fact.

Even the glow of the Christmas lights, painstakingly hung over a month earlier by Luke, wasn't enough to power through the churning flakes. A whiteout, indeed. "Coach is having practice in this weather?" Gretchen wondered aloud. She'd known Luke Hart from when she was in high school and he was the resident heartthrob teacher. Though ever since they'd hired Gretchen, he'd told her time and again to call him Luke, she'd never shake *Coach*.

"It was their last weight training session before Christmas," Gretchen answered. "Indoors, naturally. In the high school gym. He was supposed to be done by now." She glanced at her wristwatch. "I'd better phone him. Be sure he's safe. His athletes, too."

Gretchen lowered into the armchair at the window, mesmerized by the weather, unable to tear her gaze away. When she'd left the farm, the snow had stopped altogether, but the sky had hung heavy and dark, and the wind was picking up. Amazing how just a span of half an hour could bring a small town to its knees, immobilizing everyone. Freezing them, so to speak.

Gretchen wondered if this sort of thing made some people feel trapped. No doubt her mother did. Maggie was a goer. A mover and shaker and although she'd stuck around Hickory Grove, she always had things to do and places to be. Her preference for bebopping around town, as she said, partially came from the fact that she worked out of the home. She'd even cautioned Gretchen against following in her footsteps. *You'll grow antsy, trust me. Working at home sounds great until you're stuck there, eight hours, trapped in your house like a slave to the biz. Don't get me wrong, Gretch, I love it! But I'm just warning you.*

Gretchen would have *loved* to stay in her little barn house all day. By no preference of hers, she was the antithesis to her mother, running here and there and home so rarely that the space had yet to *really* feel like home. She'd never even had a friend over to watch a movie or dinner, save for Theo. He was old news, though.

But old news or not... the mere thought of him drove a chill up her arms and a cold stab to her heart. His stupid text, luring her back. She'd resist Theo Linden. She had to, if her pride mattered one lick. Theo had two more years at N.D. Then law school, wherever that took him. They would have been doomed to keep long distance, or else she'd play tag-along while he gallivanted in and out of hip college bars with his hip college friends and fancy college lingo. Meanwhile, back at what might have been their sterile apartment, Gretchen would be playing house, setting the table for a boyfriend who had better things to do than propose to his small-town, small-beans girl.

At least, this was Gretchen's fear. In reality, Theo and

Gretchen never much moved past weekend date nights. They'd never been serious. Didn't get that far. Her walls were up, and his time was limited.

Despite it all, however, Gretchen missed Theo. Her stomach twisted and she tore herself away from the window, returning to the front desk, where she'd left her handbag. She opened it now, removing her mother's stocking. She still had to do the exterior stitches to make it look old-fashioned and handmade. The latter of which, it was. Still, she was going for *neat and clean but quaint and charming*. Big, looping stitchwork around the edges of the stocking as if a child had tried her hand at sewing for the first adorable time.

Gretchen threaded a fresh needle and punctured the fabric just as Miss Liesel returned from the kitchen. "The weather is bad in Michigan, too," she declared. "Artic blast or some other thing. Although, Michigan knows how to handle it. I bet they are sending flights."

"You said you have family there?" Gretchen inquired out of politeness. In truth, she wasn't that interested in the woman's travel plans. Liesel Hart had the reputation of being prickly and perfect and *together*. Everything that Gretchen wasn't.

"Distant relatives," she answered.

Greta rejoined them. "I just got off with Luke. He's stuck. Though he's got the truck, there are five kids there with folks who can't come get them. I suppose it's just us girls for the evening." She smiled hopefully, and Gretchen felt a bit sorry for the woman. Greta hadn't made much headway with friends in town. Sure, Gretchen's mom, Maggie, and Theo's mom, Becky, had been sweet enough, going so far as to invite Greta to anything and everything.

Still, though, there was a coolness between Greta and the rest of Hickory Grove. Like they didn't quite trust her.

But Gretchen trusted Greta. After all, they practically shared the same name.

"I'm going to put supper on. We've got a full house tonight, so I'm thinking pasta," Greta went on. "Do you ladies prefer red or white sauce?"

Gretchen's stomach growled. "White," she said.

"Really," Miss Liesel answered, her face filled with worry, "I can't stay. I'll be on my way as soon as this lets up."

Gretchen glanced through the front window. "I don't know about that, Miss Liesel. You might have to make other plans. At least through the night."

"The rooms are booked," Greta said, wringing her hands. "But you can stay in the main house." Her face then lit up. "With me and Tabby, assuming Luke doesn't return. Then again—I don't see how I can walk Tabby out through this. Even just fifty yards."

"Why don't we all set up in the parlor?" Gretchen suggested. "It's warm in there. Comfortable, too. We can cancel the evening sherry and close the parlor. I'll bring down blankets and pillows from the linen closet. We'll roast marshmallows!"

Liesel sucked her red lips into her mouth then pushed them out into a pout before glancing yet again through the window. "Oh, all right. All right. I suppose we'll hunker down."

Gretchen couldn't help but smile when she saw relief play out across Greta's face. This could be just the boost Greta Hart needed. The chance to bond with a certified Hickory Grove native. The chance to find some common ground.

The burst of hope that filled Gretchen's heart also inspired her to take out her phone. While there was no way in the world she'd *reconnect* with Theo, she could at least be polite. Civil, even.

"*Welcome home*," she wrote, pausing as she considered what next to write. Logically, small talk was her best bet. "*I'm at the Inn. Bad storm. Are you safe at your mom's?*"

He wrote back immediately. "*She sent me to stay with Mamaw at the farm. You need anything? I've got four-wheel drive...*"

No, Gretchen did not need anything at all.

"Oh dear," Greta said as she emerged from the storage room behind the front desk. They stored cleaning supplies and extra toiletries there, along with a small stack of firewood for emergencies.

"What?" Liesel asked.

"We're low on wood."

CHAPTER 4—LIESEL

Gretchen shook her head. "Coach split half a cord the other day. It's all stacked and ready out back —" Her voice fell away. "Oh." There was no getting to the wood that sat way out at the back of the garden. Not now. Though the weather had been snowy and cold all day, they only sometimes had fires. For example, they'd have one the next night—Christmas Eve, for the guests during supper or after. As such, there sat just enough firewood for an evening's worth. With a working furnace, there was no point in wasting good firewood now.

But then, the furnace only held out as long as the electricity did.

As if on cue, the lights blinked on and off for the second time that evening.

Liesel frowned. Sure, they had the option of heading outside and into the storm. The back garden was just fifty yards off or so. She could do it, if she had to. Gretchen would help. Greta, too. They were tough women. All three could bundle up and press out through the swirling snow.

Crack.

Tabby started to wail. The lights blinked again then died.

"Oh, heavens," Greta fretted as the room darkened. She shushed Tabby. "I don't think we've ever had the electric go out since we've owned this place."

Liesel's eyes adjusted to the very dim light—a glow coming from the snow outside. She spoke next. "When the power went out when my mother lived here, we'd just light candles. If it was cold, then the fire. But now we will have to go out for wood. Right?"

Greta nodded just as footsteps sounded from above. Liesel glanced up, staring hard through the darkness.

The guests.

"Oh, come on down everyone!" Greta called up before directing her attention back to Liesel and Gretchen. "There are candlesticks in the junk drawer in the kitchen. Matches, too. Gretchen, won't you go on and light one up and come back." Then she lifted her voice again, and Liesel moved toward the staircase, doing the one thing she could do with ease on her phone, turning its flashlight on and lighting the stairs for the small, confused group of people.

A full house at the inn meant five parties. Five rooms, five parties. In this case, on December 23, most of the guests were singletons, in the area to meet up with family or perhaps on business nearby. What with so many hotels and motels booked for the week, the Hickory Grove Inn easily became a good back-up plan for travelers. Quaint and all-inclusive, one could scarcely argue against the merits of the small-town B&B.

Of the six people descending the steps, four were individual guests. One was a couple in town for family Christmas. None complained. Mainly, they were just curious.

"In case of times like this, our first goal is to keep

everyone safe," Greta announced. Tabby had fallen back asleep, no longer roused by the loud storm. The hubbub had worn her out. It was wearing Liesel out, too.

Once the small group joined them in the lobby, Liesel crossed back to Greta and offered her arms for Tabby. Greta passed the baby over carefully, and Liesel left to the rocking chair that sat in the parlor near the threshold to the foyer, so that she could hear the goings on while keeping Tabby down.

"Here you go," Gretchen whispered, a single white candlestick aglow behind her cupped hand.

"Thanks, Gretch," Greta answered. "As I was saying. You are welcome to stay down here if you'd prefer. We don't currently have a fire on, but we'll get to that soon, I expect. If you're cold, we have plenty of blankets to go around. Bottled water. Other drinks, too. Mainly, I think we just stay in," Greta added emphatically. Liesel wondered if this was for her benefit, even though by now it was a foregone conclusion that she'd have to stay.

The four businessfolks muttered and eventually retreated upstairs, unfazed, it would appear, by such a catastrophe. The couple, middle-aged and mainly bored, lingered long enough for Gretchen to walk them upstairs, where she'd get extra blankets. After, Gretchen brought up the bottled water and reminded guests to let their loved ones know they were safe but might be out of touch, assuming their phones died eventually. Although, the phone line was still in working order, just in case.

Then, it was the three women and Tabby again, in the parlor.

"Okay," Greta went on, her face marred by worry. "I got back in touch with Luke and there's more bad news," she confessed.

"More bad news?" Liesel frowned and glanced back through the window. The snow hadn't let up, and a fresh blast of wind whipped snow into the window long enough for her to see swirling white from here to the North Pole.

"The wood—he said he didn't tarp it."

"Didn't tarp it?" Gretchen asked, fear creeping into her voice. "So, it's wet?"

"It'll be wet, yes. I mean, it's not a *big* deal. We have blankets. I'm just—well, it's Tabby. Mainly I just want to make sure she doesn't catch her death of cold."

Liesel, ever pragmatic, pursed her lips. "We'll keep her bundled tight. She'll be fine."

"No matter," Greta added, a modicum of joy coloring her voice. "He's sending help. Though he's got to stay with his athletes, he called a friend to come over and deliver some essentials."

"In this weather?" Liesel pressed. "I thought it wasn't safe to drive."

Greta shrugged. "Luke's worried about the baby," she added. "He's sort of freaking out. I need more formula for Tabby. I don't have extra here. It's in the main house. And diapers, too."

"Well, where is the friend coming from? Is he far? Are we sure it's safe?" Liesel felt more disgruntled now, knowing that there was help on the way but that she, herself, couldn't just jump in her car and take off. Then again, it was only a car. She didn't know how to put chains on. It was probably a miracle she'd made it to the Inn at the time she did. The roads wouldn't be cleared in the near future and darkness was sweeping across the town.

"I texted someone, too," Gretchen chirped quietly.

"What?" Greta asked. Her face twisted deeper into concern, and Liesel realized that this was the first crisis she'd dealt with as an innkeeper. A small crisis. At least, for now. But her first, and the first was always the hardest. Liesel knew about crises. She'd had her share—either directly or indirectly.

"I freaked out. I mean, I didn't know the wood wasn't tarped, but I figured we couldn't make it out to the stack. What if Tabby gets cold, like you said? What if we get cold? Or the guests? And what about the marshmallows?"

"Do you even have marshmallows on hand?" Liesel asked, half-joking.

But Gretchen nodded seriously. "I always have marshmallows on hand."

"Fair enough. So, who did you text? What are they bringing?" Greta asked.

"He's bringing wood," Gretchen said. "As much as he can."

Liesel narrowed her gaze on Gretchen. "It's that Linden boy, isn't it? What's his name?"

"Theo," Greta offered helpfully. "But, Gretchen, I thought you two broke up?"

"We did," Gretchen announced firmly. "But we're still —*friends*."

Liesel studied the pretty young girl carefully. She'd never heard someone pronounce friends in that way. So fraught. So *filled.*

Liesel, herself, had rarely befriended men. In her estimation, there was no such thing as opposite-sex "friends."

"You care about him," Greta pointed out. "That's clear."

"And he cares about *you*," Liesel added.

Gretchen's eyes widened and her hand flew to her cheek. "Well, sure. I mean—we... we're close. We'll always be close."

Greta clicked her tongue. "I don't know why you two

broke up. No one in Hickory Grove does. You were... you two were meant to be together, if you ask me."

Liesel knew Greta meant this. Greta was a romantic. A lover and a kisser type. Unlike Liesel herself, who'd so rarely enjoyed the serious company of a man. What was Gretchen like?

In some strange way, Liesel saw her own mother in Gretchen. She seemed... self-sufficient. Hardy. Capable and strong but soft, too. Liesel tried to swallow the memory down. But it wouldn't go.

STEP 2: CUT THE PATCHES

H er mother shifted around fabric and tools and joined Liesel on the wooden bench. "Now for cutting. This is a critical step, Liesel."

"Isn't the critical part stitching everything back together?" Liesel didn't mean to be obstinate. But it was her nature, of late, to question everything her mother said. An aftereffect of adoption, some thought. The adopted child pushed back. Hard.

Her mother shook her head. "After understanding the rules of quilting, you have to understand somethin' else. You can't patch fabric together if it's already whole, sweetheart. And, well, if you don't already have scraps, then you make them."

"That seems silly," Liesel pushed again. "Wasteful, too. Why don't we just work with scraps so we don't waste any fabric?"

Her mother seemed to consider this for a moment. "Sometimes, a yard of fabric sits around for a long while. It's not a scrap, necessarily, right? A whole yard or two of fabric could make any number of things. It could be anything in the world, I'd reckon."

Liesel blinked.

Her mother went on. "But then again, it's just been sitting

around, and now, Liesel, isn't that a waste? Why not take that good fabric and make it somethin' more useful?"

This made sense, Liesel had to admit. She nodded. "Sure. So, you take the good fabric and break it down to make it something new. Why do we have to cut it into such little pieces, though?"

"The little pieces become our patches. They'll get reborn, you could say. As a pretty new block. You'll see. Now, watch here. We only need to work with two of our fabrics. The red and the cream. We'll cut squares. See, here, Liesel. This is the first patch. We'll cut two. And this second, we'll cut two again. The third, we cut four, and the fourth we cut one."

"It's a lot of numbers to keep track of." Liesel wasn't one for numbers.

Her mother laughed, that soft warm laugh. They each took a brief break to sip from their cocoa then got down to it: measuring, marking, and cutting. A slow and thoughtful process. Liesel still questioned if this really was the most critical step, but despite her wonderings, she trusted her mother.

In time, they'd finished their cuts, enough to make that first block.

"How many of these will we make?" Liesel asked.

"You mean the blocks?" Her mother pressed her lips together and lifted one eyebrow. "Depends on the size of the blanket. Are we making it for a king size bed? A lot. A baby quilt? Not as many."

"Let's just do a baby quilt," Liesel answered, laughing nervously.

Her mother smiled. "Do you know any babies who need a blanket?"

"Babies always need blankets," Liesel figured aloud.

"That's true." Her mother stood and reached for her pin cushion.

"*Anyway,*" Liesel went on, "*someone else will have a baby eventually.*"

"*Maybe even you,*" her mother prodded, eyeing her. "*One day.*"

This was a touchy subject between them. Once her mother had confessed that Liesel and her brother were adopted, pressure descended on the family. Pressure to pretend it didn't matter. That they were still and truly a family. Pressure not to ask about their biological roots. Pressure to remain faithful.

Liesel leveled her chin. "*I won't have children.*"

"*Sure, you will,*" her mother replied. "*One day, you'll find your match in this world, and then you'll have your own precious baby to bounce.*"

"*What if I can't though?*" Liesel frowned at the thin slices of fabric in tiny piles.

Her mother felt this question in the gut, clearly. She rocked back on her heels then lowered down to the bench, where she took Liesel's hand. "*In life, women are meant to be mothers, Liesel.*"

"*If that's true, then how come God made it so you couldn't have your own kids?*" Liesel felt the threat of tears at the back of her throat. She swallowed hard, her nostrils flaring.

Her mother laughed again, but it was still soft and warm. She squeezed Liesel's hand. "*Women don't have to carry babies to be mothers. We're naturally mothers. All the time. In many ways. Just as I am your mother, and just as the woman who had you is also your mother.*"

"*I can't have two mothers,*" Liesel argued, her tears dissolving to near-anger.

Her mother's face grew serious. "*Liesel, listen to me. The woman who had you is your mother. She cared for you while you grew inside of her. You just don't remember it. And then, for whatever reason in the world, she knew that it was right for you to have me. And for me to have you.*"

"Kind of like Bess," Liesel answered, grappling for anything to pull her out of the pain brewing in her chest.

Bess was their dog. A golden retriever who'd been spayed too young and had incontinence issues to the point of being an outside dog much of her life. She came in when she wanted, sure. But as if she knew she couldn't manage well enough, she kept to the yard and garden, sometimes wandering up to the back shed or over to the Inn next door. A couple of years earlier, a mama cat had a litter of kittens in the woodshed and never returned. Bess took the kittens, one by one, to the house where Liesel fawned over them. She went to the market, purchased bottles and sweet milk and together, she and Bess brought up those kittens until they turned into good helpers at the property, thwarting off rodents and curling around the legs of visitors, languid and fat and happy.

"Yes," her mother answered. "Just like Bess. And you, too. Together, you took over for that mother cat, right? That's what women do, Liesel," she added, tucking a strand of Liesel's golden hair behind her ear. "They mother."

CHAPTER 5—GRETCHEN

Gretchen rocked Tabby in her arms until Greta returned to take the fussing baby. She liked being a mother's help to her employer. She knew that mothers needed help. Her own mother had, after all, and she was happy to give it.

More reluctant, however, was Gretchen when it came to *accepting* others' help.

In fact, she regretted accepting Theo's help. Especially once Greta and Liesel raised their eyebrows at her. But he wouldn't be around for half an hour. He had to load up and then the drive would take longer than the usual ten minutes, no doubt.

In that time, she grabbed her stocking and returned to the parlor with Liesel.

Greta swept Tabby to the kitchen to prepare the last of the formula for her, now that she was up and fussing again. Bedtime for the baby would come a bit later, but with fresh formula en route, Greta claimed she was safe to use what she had.

"You sew?" Liesel asked Gretchen as she hunkered closer

to the single lit candle in the parlor. Greta had lit the other candles and used one to light her way to the kitchen and set about her work in there.

Gretchen flushed at Liesel's question. "Hardly. I'm learning, but it's slow. Between my two jobs and responsibilities at home, I only get a little time here and there."

"You did that stocking all by hand?" Liesel leaned closer to Gretchen, who found the courage to show the woman.

"Oh, no. I have an old Singer. It was my great grandmother's. At least, I think it was. I cut the pattern and ran it through. Now I'm just adding these stitches for show."

"Embellishment," Liesel said, and a smile lifted her entire face. Gretchen wasn't sure she'd seen Liesel smile all night.

Encouraged, Gretchen nodded. "Right, yes. I crochet more often, though. I started crocheting years ago, when I was just a girl. I've always loved crafts."

"I do, too," Liesel answered. "In fact, it's my main hobby."

"You sew? And craft?"

"Mostly I like to quilt. It got me through some hard times, you know."

Gretchen considered this. She didn't know Liesel, but the polished look and pretty style certainly didn't indicate she'd suffered much in life.

Then, Gretchen wondered how people saw her. Did they see the hard times on her face? In her clothes? Her makeup? Or did they think she'd had it easy just as Gretchen figured Liesel had.

Gretchen had never been like her mother—not a hairdresser type who was good at playing therapist, at pulling people's demons out and washing them down the drain or snipping them away—*only half an inch, though! Just a trim.*

But it felt a lot like Liesel *wanted* to be asked about it.

"Hard times?" Gretchen said simply, emulating what she'd seen Greta do over and again. Just repeat what the other person said. *It suggests you need clarity because you're confused, not nosey.*

Liesel eased back into her chair. "Sure. All women have hard times. All *people* do."

"And you like to quilt?" Gretchen was careful to preserve the conversation without being rude or intrusive.

"It's what I do," Liesel answered, smiling mischievously.

Gretchen desperately wanted to answer in kind. That crafting or quilting was what *she* did, too.

But she was still curious about the hard times. Especially on a woman who seemed, well, so perfect.

"I've had hard times, too. Like you said," she replied.

"With your breakup?" Liesel asked.

Gretchen blew air through her lips. "No. Much harder than that."

"You mean it wasn't hard to end your relationship with Theo?" Liesel asked, her tone... *knowing.*

Gretchen frowned. "Well, it wasn't easy, I suppose. But I've had harder days than that. Anyway, like I said, we're still friends. So..."

"I see. It's not technically *over*. That's why it's not hard?" Liesel's smile remained, but there was a coolness in her gaze.

Unafraid of a small challenge, Gretchen took the bait. "We are over. Yes. My hard times had more to do with my parents' divorce. Scrimping by. That sort of thing. I had to help when my siblings were born, and that was hard, too." She felt unreasonably defensive. It was becoming patently clear that Liesel didn't know a thing about hard times. Gretchen bristled and lowered her head as she stabbed the needle back through the stocking.

"That is hard," Liesel answered, her voice softening. "I don't know what it's like, though. You're right about that."

Gretchen glanced up, her needle and thread moving with her eyes. Then, she looked back at her stocking, swooping the thread around and working it back through, soothed by the motion. "Everyone goes through hard things. No one's is harder than another's."

"Hm," Liesel replied, non-committal. "You're a natural at that." She indicated at Gretchen's lap by a nod of her head. "You worked for the seamstress uptown, right?"

"That's right," Gretchen replied. "I did the laundry and pressed garments. Nothing important."

"Washing and pressing are incredibly important. Especially in quilting. Have you ever learned?"

"To quilt?" Gretchen glanced up then back down and shook her head. "No, but I've always wanted to. I'd like to be able to do it all. Crochet, knit, sew, quilt. Like I said, it's my passion."

Liesel replied, "It used to be mine, too."

Gretchen's curiosity piqued. "Used to be?" She laid down her project, giving Liesel her attention.

"Yes. It was my savior, so to speak, when I was considering my vocation. No matter what avenue I tried, nothing stuck. I never met someone, so that eliminated becoming a homemaker or a stay-at-home-mother, from which I've probably never quite recovered." She laughed lightly. "That was my dream as a girl. To have my own daughter one day and do all those mother-daughter things my own—my own *mother* did with me." Her voice cracked and she cleared it. "Anyway, I tried my hand at various professions or *vocations*. That's what we call our professions in the Church. The Catholic faith, I mean. We try to nail down our God-given gifts and then... well... do those things. The problem was, I never could nail down my God-given gifts. I just sort of assumed that my God-given gift was to be a wife and a mother."

"You could have adopted," Gretchen pointed out inquisitively.

Liesel shook her head. "I actually tried. Turned out the state of Indiana frowns upon single mothers looking to adopt. They preferred married couples, and there were enough of those to go around. I didn't have enough money to push the matter, so I put in for fosters. That didn't pan out, either, and that's when I gave the Sisterhood a go."

Gretchen frowned. "The Sisterhood?"

Liesel smiled and glanced towards the kitchen as if it was a secret she was about to share. "I was once going to become a nun."

For whatever reason, this caught Gretchen entirely off guard, and she couldn't hide her surprise. "A *nun*?" Gretchen may not have gotten serious with Theo... and it was true that she had no other prospects, but she couldn't imagine a chaste life. Devoting herself to the Church like that seemed extreme.

"Yes, I figured you'd think I was crazy."

"Not crazy," Gretchen protested. "Just... I've never personally known a nun. I mean, I've *known* nuns, but I never knew someone who—"

"Who wasn't a nun all your life? You never knew someone who wasn't a nun then become one. Or maybe vice versa," Liesel offered.

"Yeah. I suppose that's it. It's certainly uncommon, too."

"It used to be less so. When I was a young girl, the convent was a viable option. One to seriously consider, and not only if you couldn't marry. Back when my mother was a child, it wasn't rare for one of her friends to aspire to serve God in that way."

Gretchen returned to her stitching, trying hard to act casual in the face of what was becoming a borderline uncomfortable conversation. She wasn't accustomed to talking about such personal topics, especially with a veritable stranger. A loud wash of blizzardy wind barreled against the house. Gray-white masked the window as the storm whipped against it loudly. Tabby fussed in the kitchen. Gretchen wondered who it was that Coach was sending. And when Theo would arrive.

"What do you think changed?" she asked Liesel, knotting a line of thread and snipping it. "I mean, how come girls don't consider the Church more often these days?" Gretchen knew the answer. And it had to do with the thing that scared her most about getting serious with Theo. Those particular expectations of young love. Or lust, as was more often the case. Call her old-fashioned or naïve, but Gretchen wasn't one to *play house*, and that's what she worried about with Theo and the long-distance thing. One thing could lead to another, temptation would take hold, and then...

Though he never did pressure. Not once. Maybe that scared Gretchen, too. The "too-good-to-be-trueness" of it all.

"It's not what you might think," Liesel answered, her lips curling again.

Gretchen felt herself flush. "I don't know what you mean," she answered, focusing all her attention on threading the needle with a new color of thread. Green.

"I think this next generation has trouble with commitment. And while divorce continues to become more and more socially acceptable and a desire to wait on marriage becomes trendy, that still isn't it, either. And it's not the hard work, mind you." Liesel shook her finger, the clean, manicured red nail flashing in the low glow of the candlelight. "It's always more. More and bigger and better and newer and different. And that flies in the face of Christianity."

Gretchen considered this. Having only ever been a casual church goer, she really didn't have a leg to stand on in arguing against Liesel. Still, something occurred to her that the woman might consider. "That's not entirely true," she said carefully, eyeing Liesel discretely from the corner of her vision. "I think Christians desire to love God more and bigger and better. And faith is all about newness. New life. New chances. Different paths." She blinked and looked up at Liesel, who'd cocked her head. Her mouth had fallen slightly agape.

"I never thought of it that way," she murmured, her brows knitting together in consternation. Then, she shook her head. "I didn't become a nun for a different reason anyway."

"Oh?" Gretchen looked back at her stocking. She was nearly done with this. Dakota's would be next. Then her sister's. She might finish them all tonight. "So, what happened?" she asked.

Three sharp raps sliced through their conversation.

Someone was at the door.

Greta smiled. "Essentials are here."

CHAPTER 6—LIESEL

L iesel peered curiously at the front door, fully expecting Gretchen's so-called *friend* to appear.

But it wasn't Theo Linden. It was a different man.

"Coach Ketchum," Greta breathed his name on a shutter of relief and passed the baby to Gretchen, but Liesel remained frozen on the threshold between the parlor and the foyer, useless.

Snow whipped around him as he twisted inside, his arms laden with snow-capped paper grocery sacks. Once in, he shook his head like a wet dog.

Liesel narrowed her stare on him. For being her same age, Mark Ketchum was easy on the eyes. A fit figure—the perk of being a coach—and full head of hair helped to give him a one-up on many of his contemporaries.

"Ladies," he said as Greta pushed the door shut and secured the deadbolt as if the snow had the power to break in. "Don't go out there. I'm glad Luke called me. I—" he stammered as his eyes focused on Greta, then Gretchen and the baby, and at last to the stairs, where half the guests had emerged again, interested in the goings-on of the first floor of their storm-straddled B&B.

"Hello," Liesel said at last, crossing the threshold, both feet now squarely on the hardwood floor of the foyer.

Liesel's eyes hung briefly on Mark and his on her.

"Miss Hart," he answered. "Didn't expect to see you here tonight." The words sank like a heavy brick in the quiet house. Quiet, save for the blizzard outside.

She pushed her lips into a pout. "Likewise." She tried for a smile but then remembered she hadn't touched up her lipstick. There was every chance it had bled into the cracks at the sides of her mouth. Or worse, onto her teeth. She ran her tongue over her teeth only to feel the gesture come across as lascivious. Stopping, she simply pricked her mouth up and nodded.

Greta retrieved Tabby and her bottle from Gretchen and addressed the onlookers who'd joined them by the front desk. "Hi, all. No news yet. I did call the electric company, and a transformer is out nearby. They are standing by for the weather to die down before they can repair. It's pretty bad out there."

One of the guests hooked a thumb at Mark. "You'd think if he can make it out, a power worker could."

Liesel threw the caustic guest a sharp look then remembered her place there and softened. People were stressed. *She* was stressed. Michigan awaited her, but here she was, stuck in her nephew's little Inn with a girl who might have been a younger version of herself and a handsome high school football coach who made Liesel's knees turn to jelly and her throat close up as if she was fifteen again. Ridiculous. She wasn't fifteen. She was closer to *fifty*. And so was *he*, most ridiculously of all!

"Yes, well. Coach Ketchum is a renegade." The sweet blonde innkeeper shrugged Tabby up on her shoulder and gave Mark a severe look. "And it wasn't safe for you to come here. In fact, it's not safe for you to leave. Might as well get comfortable, Coach. If I'm not letting Aunt Liesel leave, then you can bet your bottom dollar I won't let you, either."

Mark groaned. "I can't stay, Greta. I told Luke I'd drop this by just in case." He set the bags down. "And now, I'm off. I'll drive slowly. I promise."

And without another chance to talk him down, Mark swept back out through the front door, unlocking it and tugging it shut behind himself and leaving wet white footprints from his boots on the utility mat made for just that sort of thing. Still, their presence felt foreboding in some way. Liesel shook the thought and let out the breath she didn't realize she'd been holding.

The guests who'd come down ambled into the parlor and stared hard out the window as Greta, Gretchen, Tabby, and Liesel slipped into the kitchen. There, they emptied the bags by candlelight and chatted mildly, as if they weren't trapped in a snowstorm as an innocent man took his life in his hands and drove off into a blizzard.

"That wasn't very smart," Gretchen chided, clicking her tongue. Liesel agreed silently.

"You can't tell Mark Ketchum what he can and can't do," Greta responded, pulling out a tin of formula powder and shelving it in a cupboard. "He doesn't even listen to me."

Liesel wondered if she oughtn't have either. She could be on her way to a different airport by now. Or maybe just on her way home. Maybe she wasn't listening to Greta, though. Maybe she was listening to something else.

"Anyway," Liesel added, "didn't you say Theo was

coming by with wood? Maybe you should call him and tell him to stay home."

Gretchen's eyes flashed at Liesel before she tugged her phone from her sweater pocket and swiveled away, texting furiously as Liesel peered on. She turned back just as quickly. "My phone died."

CHAPTER 7—GRETCHEN

Theo shouldn't have come. But he was there now, and even worse? He was in trouble with his *mama*. Sure, he was twenty, but in Hickory Grove, you were your parents' child until the bitter end. And that meant that a grown man could still be in trouble with his *mama*.

The four of them stood awkwardly in the kitchen. Three single white candle sticks glowed on the table. Just after the girls and the guests finished supper, he'd appeared, frosted over from head-to-toe and lugging an oversized, worn canvas tote, chock full of split wood and kindling.

Greta shushed Tabby, whose bedtime was fast approaching. Liesel poured milk into a kettle to boil for hot cocoa.

"Thank goodness for a wood-burning stove," Liesel remarked. She and Greta fussed over how many scoops of powder for each mug, and Gretchen turned to her ex-boyfriend.

Gritting her teeth, she hissed, "You can't stay here. Not *overnight*."

He shot back, "You *want* me to drive in this?"

"You drove over here, didn't you?"

"And you shouldn't have," Greta interjected, her tone sharp. "It's one thing for Mark Ketchum to drive. He's got that big truck and four-wheel drive. And he's old. You didn't have to come, Theo. It was a dangerous thing to do."

Gretchen winced as Greta admonished him. She knew her employer meant to be motherly, but then... they really *could* use the wood, and maybe they ought to be grateful.

As if reading her mind, Miss Liesel added, "But we're glad you did, Theo." Then, she winked at Gretchen, who wanted to melt into the hardwood floor like one of the snowflakes that Theo carried in on his snow boots.

"*Anyway.*" Gretchen cleared her throat. "I need to get back to work."

Greta waved her hand vaguely. "What work? The guests are fed. Dishes done. Bed turned down. Go on. You two, go. Relax."

Gretchen's skin prickled as Theo took a step near her. She glanced his way. "Sure, okay. I need to work on my sewing projects, anyway." She felt through the dark, sensing the path as she led the short way from the kitchen to the parlor.

Theo followed her with one of the candlesticks, placing it at the center of the coffee table. Before dinner, Liesel and Greta had figured out how to use the old record player in the parlor, setting a Frank Sinatra Christmas special on. It still played now, offering a gentle holiday heartbeat as a backdrop to their awkward reunion. The reunion each one of them wanted and didn't want. Then again, it was stupid of Gretchen to presume to know what Theo wanted or didn't want.

Maybe there was something to the age-old idea about men and women and being friends. Then again, Gretchen didn't really feel like a woman. So, if she wasn't a woman, if she was still a girl—and in so many ways, she *was*—then maybe there could be a friendship. Something innocent and devoid of want. Devoid of all the things that threatened the balance of what she and Theo had carved out before she called it quits.

"I'm sorry, Gretchen," he mumbled once she took her place back in the floral print sitting chair. "Jingle Bells" turned to "Silent Night," and Gretchen felt sad suddenly. Here she was, hours before Christmas Eve, with one stocking done, no gifts bought, and at least three stockings to go. Maybe more, depending on if she could pull it off. And not only that, she was now officially locked in a snow-embedded inn with her ex-boyfriend who she was never very serious about but who she never *officially* got over.

As if the song change really was an omen, Gretchen realized she hadn't heard the wind in a while. Maybe since before supper.

Then, as soon as she realized that, the lights flickered on, buzzing then *boom. On*, on. She felt naked under the glimmering parlor chandelier. The furnace also roared to life. Cheers came from above them—the guests.

Liesel appeared in the archway. "I don't want to bother you, but there's a bit of good news."

Gretchen smiled. "Let me guess. The power came back on?"

The woman cocked her head. "Ready for your hot cocoa?"

"Well, now that the power is on, maybe I can go. Or... *should* go." Theo stood and shoved his hands in his pockets. "I'll leave the wood here. Just in case."

He shuffled to the front door, and Gretchen stood, swallowing, frowning.

Liesel gave her a look then disappeared back into the kitchen before calling over her shoulder. "Not before hot cocoa!" she called back, then bobbed her head back through the door, catching Theo before he'd crossed the threshold to the foyer. "And if you leave, I'll call Becky."

CHAPTER 8—LIESEL

Just because the power returned didn't make it safe to drive. Not for Theo, and not for Liesel. At least, according to Greta. By then, it was getting late, and Liesel had accepted that she'd best hunker down in the parlor.

However, the snow had died down enough for the little group to make their way back to the main house, should they need to.

Technically, Gretchen was to cover the late shift, which, as Greta explained, meant she'd stay until midnight. At that point their other innkeeper would arrive and take over until six in the morning. However, that plan was dead in the water—or snow, as the case may be.

This meant, that Gretchen, like Liesel and now Theo, would have to stay the night, too.

Propriety demanded, however, that Gretchen and Theo, who were already acting awkwardly enough, were kept separate.

So, the girls ended up back in the house, the innkeeper's house where Greta and Luke lived with Tabby. The one

Liesel's mother had owned. Where she'd once stowed her own afghans and quilts aplenty. Many of those were now at Liesel's home, tucked for safekeeping in her hope chest. Something occurred to Liesel as she and Gretchen each climbed beneath heavy down comforters on a set of twin beds in the guest room.

The quilt.

Folded carefully and tucked in its own little carry-on was one of her more prized possessions. It was her mother's quilt: the wedding ring pattern. The one gifted to Liesel when she chose to pursue the vocation of serving God. *You're marrying the Church now. God, now. This is as good a time as any to hand this over,* Liesel's mother had said with a harumph, adding, *I thought I'd be giving this to my daughter on her wedding day.* Then she'd smiled and squeezed Liesel's hand. *Close enough.*

Liesel had spent an inordinate amount of her adulthood wondering when she'd have that conversation with her own daughter. After she turned forty, she realized she ought to consider alternatives.

Then, years after *that*, when her biological family had made its very first contact, a dim light had blinked to life. Like that one dead Christmas lightbulb that needed to be replaced, then you just gave it a little twist, and *boom*, it was in good working order again... Liesel had it. She had sisters. Sisters aplenty. Sisters she didn't know. Sisters who were younger. Sisters who might work a bit like daughters if they all put the time in.

So, once Liesel was invited to Michigan to get to know the family, she pulled that old quilt out, smoothing it on her own bed and admiring the fine embroidery. The perfect squares, nearly seamless in their execution. Other thoughts danced over her mind. What about Greta? She'd become close to Greta. And now Greta had Tabby. And Luke would appreciate that.

But then why hadn't the lightbulb blinked on for their wedding? Maybe because, despite Luke, there wasn't anything pulling Liesel and Greta together. No common thread, so to speak.

Still, she wouldn't count the sweet-natured innkeeper out. Greta was as good a candidate as any.

Then again, Greta now owned half of Liesel's mother's things anyway. She'd probably found a different wedding ring quilt hidden in the back of a closet somewhere. So, in essence, Greta had already been bequeathed quite a lot. Quite a lot of the Hart family heirlooms.

That's why Liesel had packed the quilt for her trip. Maybe she and her family there would bond. Maybe the whole trip would turn into a longer commitment. Before she knew it, New Year's Eve would have come and gone and she'd still be there, on Lake Huron in Michigan, the freezing cold, obliviously happy.

And yet... how could she?

Liesel was social enough, sure. But outgoing? Extroverted to the point of taking up in some strange place and with some strange people, and for what?

For what? To gain another address for her address book? Another recipient of her Christmas greeting cards?

And why, anyway? Why was Liesel so *interested* in connecting with people who'd given her up? Maybe, because now that her nephew—her sole surviving relative, or at least... the sole surviving relative she *knew*—was married with his own little brood, it cast a light on Liesel's own failings. Her own losses. The things she never did have.

Gretchen was snoring lightly, like a baby snores—soft and rhythmic and sweet. Liesel pulled the comforter up to her chin and snuggled down deeper. The next morning would start a new day. A fresh layer of snow. Maybe the storm wouldn't be over. Maybe her flight would *still* be cancelled.

And maybe, by then, she wouldn't want to go anyway. Maybe her mother's quilt had something different in mind.

STEP 3: ASSEMBLE THE UNITS

"You never know where a quilt will wind up," Liesel's mother said once they were ready to put together the patches.

"What do you mean?" Liesel asked, although she figured she knew.

"Quilters often gift their quilts away, right?"

"You keep some of the ones you make," Liesel pointed out.

"Yes. Rarely though. Most of the quilts we have here are passed down from my mother, and hers before her. Or even other family members. Other friends."

"Do you know who made every quilt you own?"

Liesel's mother frowned in concentration. "I reckon I do," she confirmed. "If we take them all out and spread them across the table, I could tell you who gave me which—of those ones that were given directly to me. Or the ones my own mama told me about."

"How do you know?"

This must have been obvious, because a little smirk ticked up the edges of her mother's mouth. "Oh, honey, you always remem-

ber. A pretty fabric here or a new pattern there—they stick with your heart."

Satisfied at that, Liesel looked on as her mother showed her the steps to creating the half-square triangles. It was a tedious job, and Liesel had a difficult time imagining how they'd not only compile all those half-square triangles... but then the blocks... and then the quilt itself. There was no way they'd finish in a month.

Liesel said as much. "When will we have the time to get this done before Christmas?"

Her mother just clicked her tongue. "It's winter, Liesel. No gardening to do. Scarcely any yardwork at'all. And it's the slow season, you know."

"But it's a lot of work, I think," Liesel worried aloud. "It'll take a long time, right? All your quilts do."

"From here to the birth of Christ, we've got precious little else to do, my dear."

"Christmas cleaning," Liesel pointed out. "Baking, too."

"And quilting, three," her mother answered. "Winter is quilting season, you know."

It was true, as far as Liesel could tell. They needed something to keep their hands warm and busy. Anyway, they'd be holed up in the house from now 'til March or longer. "Quilting season," Liesel echoed. "In our quilting house."

Her mother smiled at her, then ran the back of her hand down Liesel's cheek. "My quilting partner at quilting season in our quilting house."

Liesel smiled back. "The perfect project for a mother and her daughter."

"For best friends," her mom replied, returning to her work.

"Best friends," Liesel repeated under her breath as she stole a quiet glance at her mother who'd taken to pinning her triangles. She liked being best friends with her mother. But it was a worrisome thing, too.

"Mom?" she asked, a small lump forming in her throat.

"Mmhmm?" the woman answered absent-mindedly.

"I mean," Liesel went on, blinking through her thought, "what if you die?"

Her mom laughed. "Everyone dies. So?"

"Who'll be my best friend then?"

Her mother lowered the delicate fabric to the table and turned to Liesel. A sad smile spread across her lips. "By then, you'll have your own daughter, and she'll be your best friend. And so it goes, my darlin'. On down the line."

Liesel nodded earnestly. It was a good answer. Though she still worried—what if she also didn't have her own child? What if she also had to adopt someone else's baby?

But an assuring image filled her mind. Regardless of how Liesel might come to have her own little girl, she could picture it:

A generational series of best friends and quilt makers until the end of time. And Liesel? She was but a snowflake in the progression. A little white stitch, linking the women before her to those who came after.

And that was enough.

But for now, she had her mom. Her best friend. And that was all Liesel really needed.

CHAPTER 9—GRETCHEN

Although the snow had stopped, the next morning was no less cold. Heavy gray skies froze Hickory Grove as Gretchen and Liesel woke up together in Greta's spare room.

It was a little awkward but also a little fun. Like a sleepover. Gretchen hadn't had many sleepovers in her life. A lonesome sort, she always got scared and called her mom to come get her. Or left before it was time to claim a spot on some strange family's living room floor. Gretchen preferred the smells and shadows of her own house. Back then, that was the house on Pine Tree Lane. The one they'd had to give up when things soured between her parents.

Now, as an adult who'd only recently moved into her own space, Gretchen had gotten better at sleeping in unfamiliar locales. Not, however, with unfamiliar faces to which to wake up.

As her eyes cracked open, she rubbed sleep away to see Liesel untucking herself from her bed. Incredibly, she looked just as put together as the evening before. Without makeup, however, Liesel was even prettier. Younger, too.

Light freckles splayed across her nose. Her hair, unsmooth now and crimped in wild wires, still fell into place once she'd lifted her head from her pillow. Her red nails intact, she pressed the pads of her fingers beneath her eyes then, almost mischievously, Liesel smiled at Gretchen.

"Good morning."

Gretchen pushed up and rubbed more sleep from her eyes. She could feel her hair standing on ends, staticky and crinkled. "Morning," she answered. Her mouth was dry, and she longed for a cup of hot, black, sweet coffee. Her one dietary staple.

"I need coffee," Liesel murmured, reading Gretchen's mind.

Gretchen followed Liesel downstairs, where Greta was up and at 'em, with Luke manning a simmering pan of bacon. He'd made it home just an hour before, he announced. Gretchen could see he was sleep-deprived but chipper. Tabby babbled to herself in her swing, and, all things considered, it was a picturesque family moment. If she let her mind wander, Gretchen could see herself in this way in the distant future. Maybe with someone like Theo.

Maybe with Theo.

As if on cue, the back door swung open, a frigid wind slicing into the kitchen. Theo stood in the same outfit he'd worn the night before. His eyes landed on Gretchen, and her heart stopped briefly.

She knew how she looked and how he probably saw her, standing there in the same outfit *she'd* worn the night before, too. Now without the mask of any makeup or brushed hair. Like the abominable snowman. Possibly worse.

Greta reached to Theo and took an empty plate from him. "Thanks, Theo." She turned to the others. "Theo delivered the first batch next door. You girls slept in."

Gretchen blinked and searched for a clock. It was after eight. They *had*.

"Merry Christmas Eve," Theo said, grabbing two mugs for coffee and tipping them toward Gretchen and Liesel. "I know how Gretchen takes hers. Miss Liesel? Sugar and cream?"

Liesel glanced at Gretchen, and a smile twitched across her bare lips. "Just sugar, please."

"I can help clean up after breakfast next door, Greta. Then I'll need to be on my way. Lots to do for tonight."

"Oh, that's right," Greta answered. "The tree lighting."

"Tree lighting?" Gretchen frowned. "I'm not sure if we're going. What with Rhett at home, we might just have a little family thing."

"You have to go to the tree lighting," Theo said, his voice low. "Everyone goes."

Greta cocked her hands on her hips. "She's going. Her whole family is. I talked to your mama on the phone this morning, Gretchen. She's taking all y'all up to Fern's for the tree lighting. Then you're going back home for the usual. That's what she said, at least."

The Hickory Grove Tree Lighting was *the* annual event of the season. It more commonly took place earlier in December, but this year, Miss Fern had changed things up. Fern Gale was known for never taking down her Christmas décor, but when she declared that her front-yard event would happen on December 24th this year, the town grew restless, contemplating if they oughtn't host their own separately from hers and *earlier*, as was tradition.

But Fern had her tentacles in the community, by way of Maggie Devereux, Becky Linden, and sometimes even Liesel Hart and Greta Hart. As a formidable team, they clamped down on any uprisings. The idea this year was to direct folks from the tree lighting event to Little Flock's midnight mass, a somber and candlelit affair that fewer and fewer had been attending in recent years.

It was Fern's goal to improve turnout, and so she intended to usher tree lighting goers directly to the little old Church on the corner of Main Street. This was her way. And as the local queen of Christmas, people were sure to obey.

But Gretchen's mother had been only casually religious, and she'd passed that habit onto her children, too, who moaned and groaned any time Maggie got a hankering to head to the house of the Lord.

Gretchen, though, didn't mind. She found it peaceful there, among the wooden pews and rich incense. The quiet. The echoing of the priest's homilies and the choral singing. It was peaceful. Warm.

"I'll have to touch base with my mama," Gretchen said, joining Greta at the sink. "See about our plans. Need any help?" She changed the conversation quickly.

Greta shooed her back to the table. "Sit. Sit. We all have a busy day ahead. A cold and busy day, assuming the weather lets up enough to let us move about the town. We all need our calories."

That much was true. Gretchen's stomach rumbled as Luke slid a crispy sheath of bacon onto her plate.

She looked up to see Theo staring at her. He glanced away. Gretchen's heartbeat doubled. She hated that he was seeing her like that—helpless and sleep-eyed. He stole another glance at her, and she shook her hair off her shoulders.

"Miss Liesel," she said, redirecting her focus... and Theo's. "Think you'll stick around town after all?"

Liesel leaned left to see out the window. "I haven't checked on any outgoing flights," she answered.

"The weather has lifted in Louisville," Luke offered before joining the others at the table as they began breakfast. "But Greta and I were sorta hoping you'd stay, Aunt Liesel."

"Stay?" she echoed.

"Well, sure. Come to the lighting with us. And mass. If we walked in with you, we'd probably get special seating or something." Luke grinned charmingly, and Gretchen couldn't help but giggle.

Though Gretchen was surprised to learn that Liesel had attempted in earnest to become a nun, everyone already knew Liesel as the unofficial Sister of Little Flock.

"We'll see," Liesel answered, her eyes lowered to a forkful of pancakes. "I suppose I'll need to make plans one way or another. Weather or no weather."

"Miss Liesel," Gretchen said, an idea forming in her brain. "If you *do* stay in town... will you be *busy* today?"

Liesel studied her as she chewed and swallowed then took a long sip of her coffee. "Busy? Well, only as busy as people need me to be. Why?"

"I could...I could use a little help on my Christmas gifts," Gretchen answered sheepishly. She was a fool to ask. To put Liesel Hart on the spot like that. Probably, Liesel had any number of things she'd rather do than sew up poorly cut stockings for some silly family out on the edge of Hickory Grove.

Liesel blinked, her soft, bare eyelashes fluttering as she looked again out the window. "It's Christmas Eve," she replied. Gretchen exchanged a look with Greta who shrugged.

"Do you mean you'll still go to Michigan, then?" Gretchen asked, trying to understand the woman's airy rumination.

But Liesel shook her head, and then, a smile formed on her lips. She glanced around the table, her gaze finally landing on Gretchen beside her. "It's Christmas Eve," she said again. "I'd hate to be on an airplane on Christmas Eve."

"Then stay," Gretchen urged. "Come to the lighting and to mass."

"You'll sleep here," Luke said. "Tabby would love to have you around. So would Greta." He smiled broadly. "Come on, Aunt Liesel. What's Christmas without family?"

CHAPTER 10—LIESEL

Luke had said it best. *What's Christmas without family?*

And here she was, like a desperate fool, searching out *other* family. Elsewhere. Beneath a blustery winter sky on *Christmas Eve*, for goodness' sake.

It was the answer she needed. But something was still bothering Liesel.

Something about Gretchen and the boy, Theo. Something simmering. Something that perhaps the other people in Gretchen's life had missed.

But Liesel saw.

"You need help with sewing, then?" Liesel said to Gretchen as they finished cleaning up after breakfast. Theo had left. Greta and Luke were upstairs getting Tabby ready for the big day. Liesel and Gretchen were about to part ways, too. The snowplows had come through, and the streets were drivable, if still icy.

Gretchen nodded urgently. "I got a late start, and I have nothing else to give my family. I mean—I was going to go to the market or one of the little shops on Main, but I'm worried they'll be closed today." She frowned miserably. "I'm the worst daughter ever. Sister, too."

"You're not," Liesel admonished her. "And I'd love to help. It'll keep me preoccupied enough to pass the day."

Gretchen looked at her in confusion.

Liesel explained. "Typically, I'm at the church all day on Christmas Eve. Setting up for a charitable dinner. Finishing the Foundlings giftwrapping. We sponsor families for Christmas. It's a big undertaking." Liesel frowned. "I gave up all of that this year to go to Michigan." Then, she smiled and chuckled. "I guess I feel a little... *useless* now. Out of sorts. Maybe I should find a flight after all. How awkward to show up at mass without having helped."

"Well Miss Becky and Miss Fern are helping this year, though. Right? At least, that's what I heard."

"And your mama, too, I'd imagine. Those three have become a close-knit group."

Gretchen raised her eyebrows. "I feel more and more disconnected from my own mama every day. I had no idea she'd planned for us to go to the lighting and then to mass. She spends all her time on hair or on the kids or on Rhett. I'm a little... out of touch."

"That happens," Liesel assured her. "Moms and daughters, they go through phases. She still loves you."

"I know she does. It's just—she's busy. I guess. And, well, I'm busy, too."

"And Theo?" Liesel asked delicately.

"What about him?" Gretchen shot back as she tugged her coat on at the front door.

Liesel knew this was prickly territory. If she was going to spend the day with the girl, then she'd better tread lightly so as not to make for awkwardness.

But then, it just fell out of her mouth. She couldn't hold

it back. She was desperate for something, Liesel was. Human discourse. Gossip. Sisterhood. *Something*.

"What's the story?"

Gretchen whipped her head to Liesel and they left through the door together, pausing in the cold gray Christmassy morning—Gretchen to go back up to the parking lot and Liesel to go down to the street, where she'd have to dig herself out of the plowed-in snow, no doubt.

"Do you know how to get to the farm?" Gretchen asked by way of answering the question.

Liesel let out a breath and smiled. "I'll follow you."

THE DEVEREUX FARM was a sight to behold, especially with the white shimmering blanket. Shimmering, now that the sun had peeked out between a slice of clouds at the northern most edge of the sky. The plow had made it as far as the driveway and no farther, but someone had cleared that, too, making it manageable for both Gretchen and Liesel to drive up to the space just beyond the barn.

Liesel felt awkward arriving there as Gretchen's guest. She was closer in age to Maggie, and even then, she and Maggie weren't very close.

Still, she'd promised the girl she'd help, and it was the one thing she could do and still feel good about sticking around town and appearing at Little Flock that evening.

"Come on," Gretchen waved her in. "I've got everything in the loft."

As the stepped into the weathered space, Liesel was taken aback at how homey it was. A potbellied stove anchored the room, and Gretchen was quick to add a few pieces of wood to it before getting it roaring to life. She then flicked on a space heater and rubbed her hands together. "It'll warm up quickly. Especially up there." She pointed toward a narrow, bare wooden staircase—fresh wood, it appeared. Above, indeed, sat a loft. The place and everything in it—from Gretchen's chunky knit blanket on her simple little bed, to earthen colors and handmade wreaths and garland that draped here and there—reminded Liesel not of a young woman's studio apartment.

Rather, it reminded Liesel of a... well... of a *manger*. She all but gasped as she ascended the staircase behind Gretchen.

Above, towers of fabric crowded between green milk crates chock full of scraps and supplies. A crafting house, of sorts. Not wholly disorganized, but also not quite *orderly*. At least, at first glance. Upon closer inspection, as Gretchen pulled a second folded chair from a corner and opened it for Liesel, Liesel saw that the girl had made a system. On the small sewing table—something of an artifact in and of itself—was the old Singer she'd talked about. Proper accessories sat at its corner in a ceramic bowl, handcrafted.

In many ways, not only did Gretchen's barn house remind Liesel of a manger, but so, too, it reminded her of a convent. Simple and pretty and wholesome and *necessary*. Everything there, either natural or *necessary*. And it spoke to Liesel. Truly it did.

"Wow," she breathed, glancing around one last time as Gretchen peeled a pinned pattern from a stack. The frame for her next stocking, apparently. "You have a beautiful place here," Liesel said. "Did your mother help you?"

Gretchen nodded. "When she could. I mean, she gave it to me. So that was a big help."

"What a home. It's *different*," Liesel added.

"I have a lot of work. But it's as good a home as any. I

think we'll put in a wall or two to create bedrooms. At least, that's what my mom and Rhett said."

"And you'll live here long term? Or just while you—" Liesel's question fell away as she recalled that Gretchen wasn't in college or anything. She was just—there. In Hickory Grove. Working odd jobs and saving money and handmaking Christmas gifts for her family and... *waiting*. It felt like that. It felt like Gretchen was, well, *waiting*.

Kind of like how Liesel had lived her early days. She swallowed hard.

"While I save for my business," Gretchen was quick to fill in the blank. "I want to make this place a craft store. I could hold classes here. Sell stuff, too. Maybe we could have a quilting room downstairs, even. I have big ideas, but it'll be a while. I'm not that experienced, still."

"Experience only comes with time," Liesel pointed out. "If that's what you're waiting for, then you might be waiting for a while."

"That's true," Gretchen allowed, and they got started, Liesel on the machine and Gretchen stitching the edges as she'd done to the first.

"I think Hickory Grove needs a craft store. We don't have a Hobby Lobby or a Michael's. You have to cross the river."

"Right," Gretchen agreed anxiously. "And if I can get in touch with distributors, then I can offer both locally made wares and little classes alongside the real things that crafters buy. Yarn and fabric and thread and all that. Everything that a real store has. Small quantities, maybe. But Rhett would build me a storehouse, he said. So, eventually I could expand. Maybe even have a website and sell there, too. That was Rhett's idea."

"You seem to like your mother's husband?" Liesel asked delicately.

"I like him a lot. I mean, he's not my *dad*, but he doesn't try to be. He's a good man. He makes my mama happy. He helps with the little kids, too."

"Which probably helps you," Liesel pointed out.

"That's what Theo said, too. When they first started dating, Theo reminded me that it was a good thing to have another adult around. It'd give me more free time. But he had ulterior motives."

"Ulterior motives?" Liesel echoed, narrowing her stare briefly on Gretchen before resuming her sewing.

"What did you think he wanted me to have free time for?" Gretchen rolled her eyes.

Liesel frowned. "Spending time together?"

"Exactly. He didn't necessarily care if I had free time. He just wanted my time. You know what I mean? It was self-serving, I think."

Liesel considered this as the machine hummed along. There was something defensive in Gretchen. Something broken and untrusting. Something in her that was in stark contrast to Liesel... and yet so *similar*. That inherent suspicion about people and their motives. Still, she couldn't help but point out the obvious. "Maybe so," Liesel replied. "Maybe Theo wanted your time... but is that so bad?"

"Men always want something from women," Gretchen answered. "I don't care to be a part of that sort of relationship."

"I think it's natural for young people to want to spend their time together, Gretchen," Liesel said delicately, pulling the freshly sewn stocking out from the machine and snipping the thread at the top. "That might make him self-serving, but how else do you become close to them? You both need each other's *time*. And take it from someone who knows: you don't have as much as you think." Liesel's face drew sad and thoughtful.

Gretchen clearly saw this, because she was quiet a beat. Liesel picked up the next project and started it through the machine.

"You know," she went on, "speaking of time—you mentioned you'd like to learn to quilt. And I can surely show you. You've got a great space here. We could make a plan to start on a project together."

Gretchen perked up, her eyes flashing and mouth pricking into a smile. "Really?"

Liesel grinned. "As long as you have... *time.*"

STEP 4: ASSEMBLE THE SHOO-FLY BLOCK

"The next rule of quilting is to make the time," Liesel's mother said. "We'll spend a lot of time on this. Hours each day."

"Hours every single day?" Liesel wasn't complaining. Just confirming.

Her mother smiled. "Put water on to boil. We can have some hot cocoa while we assemble the first block."

"All right, Mom." Liesel set about filling the kettle and searching for her mother's tin of cocoa powder. "And how do we do this? Do we do each block individually then put them all together?"

"That's right," her mother replied. When Liesel returned to the table, her mother had laid out their patches in rows on top of the rubber grid. Each patch sat two grid squares apart from the next on each side, and Liesel could see plain as day what the block would look like. Nine patches. Three rows by three.

"We'll stitch these units together by rows, first. Then we press the seams to set them flat toward the solid square, inwardly, you see." Her mother drew her fingers together to indicate as much.

Liesel followed. "It's not that hard."

"It's tedious, is what it is. And to lots of folks, tedious means hard."

"True," Liesel replied as they followed the next direction.

Once each row was stitched, Liesel guessed at the next step. "Now we stitch the rows together, right?"

"You're a natural," her mother complimented.

"Mom, come on. It's obvious." Liesel shook her head.

"There are a lot of little steps, though. For example, we'll make sure the seam allowance nests together. See? Anyway, it's not always obvious. Some people are too worrisome to be good at quilting."

"What do you mean?" Liesel didn't understand.

"They are so fretful they'll miss something, that they freeze up. I was that way at first. Too scared to make any progress."

"What's there to be afraid of?" Liesel asked. "It's a quilt. It isn't life or death."

"A quilt is the essence of life," her mother answered, and Liesel found this reply to be dramatic.

"And," her mother went on, "making an error, even early on can cost someone fabric and thread, and time, too."

"I can understand wasting good fabric and thread, but time— you can always spend another hour here or there."

Her mother laughed as the kettle sang out a sharp trill. Liesel went to take it off the flame and pour together the water and cocoa before she would dig around for an old bag of marshmallows, probably hard from sitting stowed for too long.

"Not everyone has a spare hour here or there. You, yourself, seemed a little hesitant to start, knowing that you'd have to commit so much time." Her mother's eyebrow rose meaningfully.

"That's true. If we had to start all over, I'd be pretty annoyed."

"But still you've got that instinct. That go-for-it-ness, my darlin'."

"You have to have a respect for the time and a heart for start-ing. That's what I always say about quiltin'."

"You sure say a lot about quilting, Mom," Liesel replied as she set two mugs of steaming cocoa onto the table.

"Ah," her mother scolded lightly. "Not on our workspace."

"Oh, right." This was a rule Liesel already knew. If her mama had a quilt on the table, there was to be no food nor drink within an arm's length. Same applied for other sewing projects, too. But quilting was particularly protected in the Hart household.

It really was *The Quilting House*, that much was true.

"For how long will we work today, Mom?" Liesel asked.

"Well," her mother answered, "we've now finished one block. Would you look at that? Now we piece it into a baby quilt. Right? So that comes next."

"Do we make more blocks first, then?"

"Yes. I reckon we do. Who knows? With the two of us working together, we might get this done in no time after all. That's the beauty of a quiltin' project. The more hands, the sooner it's done. That is, if time is of the essence."

CHAPTER 11—GRETCHEN

In less than two hours, they were done, which was a good thing, since Gretchen was running out of time. Gretchen thanked Liesel and they made a promise to get back together soon.

After, Liesel had taken her leave, heading to Little Flock to see about mass preparations, no doubt.

Liesel, Gretchen could see, was someone who was happy to give her time. Happy to have the time of others, too. Was Gretchen that way? Was she willing to share her life so easily? So quickly?

Gretchen had rarely felt selfish in her life, but with her new friend's wisdom, she began to wonder if she hadn't made a mistake when it came to Theo Linden and all things romantic entanglement.

Deep down, Gretchen cared quite a lot for Theo. And deep down, she knew he cared, too.

So, once she finished the stockings and decided to head into town to see if the corner market was open, she gave him a call. Maybe he could meet her. She could explain herself. They could be friends again.

Though not more. He still lived in South Bend, after all. He still had a year before graduation and then—two more years of law school. And who knew where that might take him?

"LOUISVILLE," he replied easily as they settled in with a set of mugs filled to the brim with Malley's famous hot cocoa and goopy marshmallows sogging on top.

"You mean—" she replied, her brows knitted.

"Yes," he finished the sentence for her. "After next year, I'm going to Louisville for law school. Assuming I get in, that is. Zack thinks I have a good shot. And he knows people, too. My grades are good. Next up is the LSAT, and then I'll have a sense, I think."

"But why? Why Louisville?" Gretchen asked then took a slow sip. She'd allotted exactly one and a half hours for her excursion. After that, she needed to get home, help get the kids ready for supper, then the tree lighting, then mass—it never ended. The hustle and bustle.

Theo chuckled. "I'm going to apprentice with Zack, for starters. I can work as a paralegal soon. But mainly, I'm transferring to Louisville to be closer to the people I love." He glanced down at his own mug, sheepish, then shook his head. "Like I said, though. I have to get in first." He took a long pull from the drink, his eyes anywhere but on her.

Gretchen took her own sip, thinking about this revelation. It could change everything.

Or nothing.

She wouldn't know, however, unless she asked. But how could she? Gretchen was the one to end things. If she went back on her word, how might Theo react? Maybe he already had a new girlfriend, anyway?

"Theo," Gretchen started, her thoughts barreling down towards her mouth, like a semi-truck whose brakes had failed and needed a safety pull-out, "um." She cleared her throat as he looked at her, his kind eyes supple. From her seat across from him, Gretchen could smell Theo. A hint of heavy cologne. What was it? Curve? Something nostalgic his mother had discovered in Grandbern's back closet, maybe. Something old and musky and warm and inviting and delicious and—

"Is everything okay, Gretchen?" Theo asked, his face hardening at the edges—his jaw tensing and his eyes narrowing.

"Yes," she rushed to answer. "Yes, everything is... fine. It's fine. Are you—Theo, are you, like... dating now?"

"Dating?" he asked, laughter at the back of his throat. "I mean, I go on dates. But nothing has stuck." He dropped his chin. "You?"

Gretchen shook her head. "Of course not."

"Why *of course*?" Theo asked. She felt his face move an inch closer to hers above the table. His elbows now rested atop it. His whole shape closed in on her, blocking out the rest of the restaurant—the rest of the *world* from her view. From her mind, even.

She could answer in a million ways. *Of course I'm not dating because there are no good men in this town.* Or: *Of course I'm not dating because I don't care about that stuff.* Or: *Of course I'm not dating because of* you.

Without warning, the last notion fell from her lips, a whisper of a truth. "Because of you," Gretchen said, managing the courage to meet his gaze. Images of their times together played through her mind. Fish frys together at Little Flock. Tailgating at the high school football games, sitting together at the edge of his pick-up truck's bed, their feet dangling. Her red toes. His law school loafers—second hand but as nifty as the starched polos he wore. Theo didn't care that he stuck out in Hickory Grove. That he wasn't a good ol' boy who'd played football for the school and could change a tire in ninety-seconds flat. He didn't care about any of that.

Did Gretchen?

"Because of me?" Theo repeated, his lower lip trembling as his eyes danced to her mouth and his face inched closer to her above the table. She felt herself inching his way, too.

She nodded slowly.

There was just one thing to do.

One thing to give Theo his answer. To give Gretchen hers.

"There he is!"

The "answer" came on a chilly breeze as the restaurant door flew open, spilling Coach Ketchum and Coach Hart inside like a pair of frozen Nutcrackers, rigid and frozen in time and space, the latter pointing directly at Gretchen and Theo. Gretchen shrank back into her seat, her cheeks reddening like cranberry sauce.

They made their way over, gloved hands and knit-capped heads laden in puffs of white snow. "Theo, Miss Fern needs help to haul out the tree, if you have a mind," Coach Ketchum said gruffly.

"Hate to interrupt you two," Coach Hart added softly. "We had another question, too."

Coach Ketchum took over, a bit less sure of himself as he went on. "Miss Hart? Liesel?" he asked Gretchen, particularly.

She frowned at first, but something inside her brain

clicked on. A softly glowing bulb. "Yes, Miss Liesel," she said, holding Coach Ketchum's nervous stare.

Beneath the table, Gretchen felt something on her foot. It took a moment to realize it was Theo. *Footsie.* Classic Theo. She caught his gaze.

"Do you know where we might, um, *find* her?" Coach Hart asked, less nervous than Coach Ketchum but just as awkwardly.

Gretchen stole herself a moment. "Why?" Then, she blushed again. "Beg your pardon, Coach. But might I ask why you want to know?"

"Oh," he coughed into his fist, contrived, then flicked a glance to Coach Ketchum. "Just curious about if she made it safely out of town. I wanted to make sure my aunt got to her destination in one piece. Haven't heard from her."

"Oh, her trip." Gretchen nodded and began to explain that Liesel's flight was grounded and that she'd stick around town for the holiday. But she was cut off.

The two men exchanged an unreadable look.

"Anyway," Coach Hart went on. "You need a lift to Pine Tree Lane?" he asked Theo. "Your mama told Greta she was worried about the weather. You desert folks not having much experience and whatnot." Theo and his mom, Becky, had lived in Arizona all of Theo's life before college brought them back to Indiana. Still, the entire reason for the coaches' visit there at the diner was clearly connected to something *other* than the tree lighting or Miss Fern needing help or *whatnot.*

"I got my truck," Theo answered.

"And you're all right, Gretchen?" Coach Hart asked, studying her more softly than he had Theo.

The air was thick around them. Liesel and Mark

Ketchum. Becky's concern for Theo. Luke Hart's concern for Gretchen...

On a whim, she rubbed the toe of her boot along the back of Theo's calf, a small smile curling on her face before she answered, "I'm great, Coach Hart. I'm with Theo."

CHAPTER 12—LIESEL

Liesel arrived at Little Flock in time to catch Fern Gale and Becky Linden *leaving*.

"Liesel!" Fern greeted. Of everyone in Hickory Grove, Liesel found herself closest with Fern. They were close in age, and their families intertwined at certain points. Plus, they were both the only pair of childless women around. Hickory Grove wasn't much for spinsters. Then again, Fern was no spinster. And anyway, she had her cat.

Liesel *was* a spinster and had *no* cat.

She smiled. "Hi, Fern. Merry Christmas." The two shared a tight hug, then Liesel offered the same to Becky.

"Merry Christmas, darlin'," Becky answered, kissing her on the cheek. "So, you're sticking around town, then?"

Liesel cocked her head. Her trip to Michigan wasn't exactly *public* knowledge. In fact, nothing Liesel did was really public knowledge. She didn't necessarily live in the public eye like some of the other locals did.

Fern must have caught her surprise. "Mark Ketchum came around looking for you."

"Mark Ketchum?" Liesel frowned. "Looking for *me*?"

Becky nodded. "And Coach Hart was with him. We were
—*are* looking for my Theo, too. We traded info with them.
They'd hunt down Theo for me—that kid never answers his
phone—and we'd keep an eye out for you." Becky smiled.
"Well, here you are."

"Did they say what for?"

Fern and Becky exchanged a look.

And by then, Liesel had an idea.

Still, it made no sense.

She and Mark Ketchum were already well enough
acquainted. And they had exactly nil in common. For him to
show sudden interest wasn't only out of the blue but also
beyond reason.

"It's the tree lighting," Fern said at last, as if letting out a
breath she'd held for a second too long.

"What about the tree lighting?" Liesel asked, now irri-
tated. "It's tonight, I know. You moved it this year."

"Right," Fern went on, again casting a brief glance at
Becky, gaining some unseen moral support. "He... he asked
if you were in town, if you would go."

"If I am in town, if I would go? He wants to know if I'll be
there?" Liesel shook her head, bewildered. "Why?"

Fern shrugged, this time without looking to Becky for
guidance. "Who knows the minds of men?"

But Becky interjected. "Well, he doesn't have family in
town, you know. He's alone at Christmas."

"He is?" Fern seemed flabbergasted.

"Oh yes," Becky confirmed. "Mark Ketchum is a hanger
on, you see."

An image came to mind. Something from years before.
Not many years. But a few. Mark. The Little Flock Community Christmas Dinner.

Her *quilt*.

"Not really," Liesel pointed out, surprised at herself for defending the man. Her nephew's colleague. Someone she hardly knew. Someone who she hoped *was* a hanger-on. At least, Liesel hoped he'd hung on to the quilt. She frowned, returning to her line of defense. "He has Luke."

"Who counts their *co*workers?" Becky asked, a touch scornful.

Fern tsked. "Plenty of people count their *co*workers as friends or even more!" she declared. "Especially those of us who have so few relatives left on this earth."

Becky winced, and Liesel's face softened. "They're good friends. Luke says so, at least. And I see Mark from time to time at the Inn. Pitching in here or there."

"It'd be nice if he swung back by here later tonight," Becky pointed out. "We'll need help with the Nativity set."

"Nativity set?" Liesel asked. "You're having the play at the candlelight mass?"

"No, earlier," Becky replied. "Maggie's directing it. It's a crazy day, I tell you." She shivered and rubbed her hands up and down her arms. "First the five o'clock mass. Then the tree lighting. Then back for the candlelight service." She frowned at Fern. "How'd I let you talk me into this?"

Fern hooked a thumb at Liesel. "Because the Queen of Little Flock was *supposed* to be out of town."

Liesel grinned. "Well, I'm here now. Put me to work."

AND WORK THEY DID. First, oiling the pews and setting up the elements of the nativity that Maggie had dropped off that morning.

After that was finished, Fern needed help at her house for the tree lighting.

"Theo should be there," Becky confirmed as each woman headed for her vehicle.

"And if Theo's there, then we know Gretchen's there, too," Becky added with a smirk.

"I thought they were old news? What, isn't Gretchen too small-town for Notre Dame's finest?" Fern eyed Liesel playfully. Liesel could see why Gretchen might have called things off. Small-town attitudes being what they were... it was a self-fulfilling prophecy that she didn't see herself in the same light Theo might have seen her. The one that shone on Gretchen when Theo turned up at the Inn the evening prior.

Becky just shrugged Fern's point away. "Long distance. It can be a real pain."

Liesel knew little about long-distance relationships. She knew about living a long distance from her biological family. The family she was supposed to reconnect with that very day. Those who she didn't know. That was about all. Not romantic entanglements of the distant sort.

Still, when Liesel, Fern, and Becky showed up at Fern's house to see Theo and Gretchen standing close—very close—on the front porch, the question was opened again.

Once everyone was tucked away inside and Fern had finished doling out orders, she caught Gretchen's elbow. "Theo?" she whispered as he and his mother left with Fern to dig out the tree trimmings from the garage.

Gretchen reddened, but her smile stretched across the whole of her face, from her chin to her eyes and out to her hands as she shook them giddily at her sides. "We're back together," she whispered in response. "We went to lunch and talked. He's here to help Miss Fern. I gotta get home to my mama and help with the kids and getting dinner on. We're eating before children's mass. Turns out Briar is playing the part of Mary. I think she'll be the youngest Mother of Jesus in the history of Little Flock."

Liesel smiled and shook her head. She missed being involved in the children's Nativity play. She'd bowed out under the assumption she'd be long gone, but still, she'd seen hints of their rehearsals on a few Sundays. She looked forward to it almost as much as she'd been looking forward to Michigan. Her smile faded as she recalled the most recent phone conversation she'd had with her kin back there. *Another time. Hopefully soon.*

"That's precious. She'll make a good Mary. I just know it."

Theo, Fern, and Becky returned, and the five of them set about decorating. There wasn't all that much to do, since Fern lived in the unofficial Christmas House of Hickory Grove. Mainly a few extra strings of lights and then the seating.

The seating and heat lamps were the biggest deal. What with the snow to contend with, it was likely folks weren't keen to hang around if there was little promise of warmth. And since it was an outdoor affair, they had to set up some warmth.

Theo set about to start up the firepit, and the ladies started with chairs, their fingers frozen as they tugged plastic from plastic and went to work.

An hour in, an SUV pulled up.

"It's my mama," Gretchen said as she let forth a heavy breath. "Time to get back to the church, I'd reckon."

"Is there anything extra you'll need?" Liesel asked as they added finishing touches on the refreshments table.

Maggi descended from her SUV, then, all long legs and wild ringlets of red hair. For being buttoned up in a winter overcoat and boots, she could have stepped out of a style magazine. That was Maggie Devereux. Sleek and cool and everything that Hickory Grove *wasn't*. And yet, she was a Hickory Grove mama, through and through.

"Gretch, we gotta *go*. Briar doesn't know her lines, and Greta is bringing the baby to the church for a quick rehearsal."

"Miss Liesel wants to know if we need anything else," Gretchen answered as she squeezed Theo goodbye, their flagrant rekindled love as infectious and inspirational as Christmas spirit itself.

"No," Maggie hollered over. "We're good, thanks, Liesel!"

And off they went.

Liesel spun around and took in the snow-blanketed front yard. Fern and Becky stood at the fire, warming their hands. Theo's face was buried in his phone. He glanced up suddenly. "I gotta go somewhere."

"Where?" Becky called over, her mother's ears ringing at panic in her son's voice.

He looked over to her and Fern then at Liesel.

"Just... *somewhere*. Somewhere on Main!" he hollered and jogged off. When he made it to his truck, he called back to the three women, "Wish me luck!"

Liesel turned back to the others. Becky and Fern clicked their tongues and shook their heads.

"That boy," Fern said as they regathered and Liesel prepared to head over to the church, too.

"He's something," Becky agreed. "Who knows the mind of a young man?"

Liesel hid her own small grin. She figured she might. At least, she knew what was on *Main* Street. Intuition kicked in.

Her face fell. It occurred to Liesel that this was the first time in the history of her making her own personal promise —her special little deal—that she was about to fail. She hadn't made it to Michigan. Nor would she. And her whole mission that year was to get there. To her roots. To see about her biological parents and be *there*. In Michigan.

She swallowed a lump down her throat and willed away the defeat, trudging to her car as she called back a farewell.

Just as soon as she got there, though, Becky Linden shouted after her.

"Liesel, wait!"

The small blonde woman half-ran, half slid down the drive toward Liesel's car at the curb. "What is it?"

Becky waved her phone. "It's Gretchen. They need something for the Nativity play."

"Oh, sure thing," Liesel replied. "I can run to the market or—"

Becky relayed this to Gretchen then put her on speaker, and she explained.

"No, no need to run to the store. We just need a little blanket. Or something like that. For the manger."

STEP 5: PIECE THE BLOCKS INTO YOUR QUILT

"We still haven't figured who we're giving this quilt to," Liesel pointed out one particularly chilly day. A fresh snow had fallen through the night, and the morning was silent and shimmery. A fresh pot of coffee brewed for the grown-ups and Liesel's mom was mixing dough for cinnamon rolls. The boys were working to get a good fire set in the parlor before they did the same next door.

"We still haven't finished the quilt," her mother answered, finishing the kneading and leaving the dough to rise before she rejoined Liesel at the table, a fresh mug of coffee in her hands.

They'd been working on the blocks for over a week, and the job was nearing its end. Between baking and household chores, the quilt had become an obsession for Liesel and her mother. They spent the mornings on it. The afternoons. The evenings. One night, each found the other, sleepless and fidgety-cold, wandering to the kitchen at the same hour in the middle of the night, and they took to a block together. When they weren't working on blocks, they were talking about shoo fly pie and the shoofly plant and how flies, as an insect, were maybe not so bad as people figured them for. Pesky, sure. But a bug that leant itself to such *sweet treats couldn't be all bad. After all, out in the country, in a small town like Hickory Grove, flies were as much the fabric of life as anything else. Then again, persistent to the core and particularly troublesome at summertime, it wasn't any wonder that they were best shooed off, even if they were likely to return.*

"Do people ever give quilts back?" Liesel asked, frowning.

"What do you mean? Like, return them to the quilter? My, I reckon, yes."

"It'd be a nasty thing to do, to give a quilt back. But maybe there are good reasons, too. Especially if the first rule of quiltin' is all about charity and so forth. Right, Mom?"

In a region of mamas, Liesel's mom was more of a Mom. Curt and practical, the woman cut a sharp image about town and in the home, both. Without an ample bosom or a thick waist, like lots of Liesel's schoolmates' mothers, Mrs. Hart's hugs weren't soft and suffocating. They were urgent and desperate. Like she was starved.

She watched her mother lay out all the blocks they'd made. Her angular features a mirror of the squares. Her thin arms and long fingers framing the small blanket as she studied it.

It was a force, that quilt. And it was just a baby blanket. For a baby they didn't even know. Maybe even a baby who hadn't yet been born. Now, that'd be something.

"A quilt finds its way to the person who needs it and to whom the quilters need to give it," her mother replied. "And if you make someone a quilt and they return it, then that doesn't say anything about the quilt or how good of a job you've done. It's just what needs to happen."

It was starting to make sense to Liesel. Like, perhaps they gave this quilt to someone with a baby, then one day, that baby grew up and the quilt was passed back to Liesel's future granddaughter or something. That'd be a return, to be sure. And a good one, too.

Still, there had to be rotten souls out there the likes of which didn't deserve a Hart Family Quilt.

"Have you ever given away a quilt and wanted it back?" Liesel pried. Her passion for the artform was so earnest, that Liesel could imagine just how many souls had earned a special quilt from her mother. Folks who didn't deserve one, probably.

"Never," her mother answered sharply. "Where's the charity in that?"

"You spend all this time on something, and then what if the person just says, 'thanks' and tosses it into the bed of their truck for a fish fry?" Liesel asked, getting the iron ready.

"Oh, Liesel," her mother answered, and suddenly, she looked older. Her face drawn, her hair silvery at the temples. "If we get to the end of this thing, and you've missed the point, then what?"

"So, you're saying then that's what the quilt was always for? A pick-up-truck-fish-fry blanket?"

"Maybe," her mother said on a breath. "And anyway, we've still got a ways until we get to that point."

"Aren't we almost done?" Liesel asked.

"Not quite. We've just got the blocks finished. Next we piece them together. Then add the batting and backing. Then we bind. Then there's one last step. At our pace, we'll finish in a week or two."

Liesel didn't mean to be obstinate, but if they finished in a week or two, they'd finish ahead of schedule by a ways. "I thought it would take us clear to Christmas. All your quilts take you forever. And you said one of the rules was time."

"We're making a small quilt, and we're working together. And," she added, giving Liesel a sharp glance, "you're good."

Liesel flushed under the praise. It never grew old, acknowledgment from her mother. Never.

"And anyway," Liesel said in agreement, "we've definitely spent time on it."

"Now, then," her mother went on, guiding Liesel to her seat. "Next step is to combine the blocks. We'll have four blocks to a row. Five rows."

Liesel followed her mother's directions, and by the time they finished joining together one row, Liesel's pancakes had cooled. Still, she gobbled them down. Quilting made her hungry.

After a load of laundry, they returned to the next row, then the next. In a couple of days' time, they'd had the top all done, and Liesel could see plain as day what the thing would look like.

It was a pretty wonder, that quilt. And still, she couldn't picture where it would wind up. Who would need it.

It was the Sunday before Christmas by the time they'd finished the batting and backing, and Liesel was due half an hour before mass.

She'd star as Mary in the Nativity play, and rehearsals were in full swing. Her lines were few, but staging and running through the lines and scenes with a hodgepodge of children of varied ages made for a mess for the Sunday school teacher who was in charge of corralling them into something resembling that special night in Bethlehem.

Once there, the teacher took stock of costumes and props. "Just five days!" Marguerite Devereux had trilled. "Five days, and we're still missing a Baby Jesus." The poor old woman clicked her tongue and shook her head as one of the Wise Men tripped on his robe and fell into a haystack.

Liesel didn't know any babies, so she was no help, there.

"What about that weird little girl who comes to Mass and sits in the front with her mama?" one of the older kids suggested—the innkeeper.

Liesel knew the girl. She reminded Liesel of a little angel. White blonde hair and transparent skin and a bizarre mother who, to Liesel's knowledge, had never once missed a Sunday in all *of Little Flock's history. Liesel's own mother sometimes sent her quilts over to the mother—Monroe, something or other.*

Liesel had even met the child and offered to babysit.

"Fern. Her name is Fern," Liesel said.

The teacher snapped. "Mrs. Monroe would be thrilled. Fern it is."

"And what about the Boy Child's swaddling clothes?" the girl who played the donkey asked. It was as good a question as any.

Something occurred to Liesel just then. She snapped her fingers, happy to be helpful twice in a row. "I have something that would work."

"What do you mean, Liesel?"

"For swaddling clothes. I have something I can bring."

CHAPTER 13—GRETCHEN

As soon as she arrived at Little Flock, she'd regretted not dragging Theo with her. Now that they were back together, with the promise of his eventual transfer to Louisville, she didn't want to be away from him even for a moment.

Her mom reined the kids together for a quick rehearsal, calling orders here and there of the older ones and of Gretchen. Briar didn't know her lines, but her Joseph did, and he helped, giving Gretchen a chance to slip away.

"Hey," a voice came up behind her from the front doors.

She swiveled, hoping to see him there. Instead, it was Coach Hart and Coach Ketchum. The latter nodded up. "Looking forward to watching this."

"You're coming to Mass?" Gretchen covered her mouth as soon as the words were out. "Sorry, Coach. Didn't mean to be rude, I just—"

"I don't always go," Coach Hart confessed, grimacing. "I guess Gretchen here assumes you wouldn't either."

"Sundays are for God and football," Coach Ketchum answered. "God first." He winked at her.

Gretchen frowned. If Coach Ketchum was a Little Flock regular, how come he and Miss Liesel didn't seem to be on closer terms? Hickory Grove was close to begin with, and folks were only made closer by the church, no doubt.

Unsure why the two were even there at the church presently, Gretchen decided it wouldn't hurt to dig a little. Then, she'd need to skedaddle home to get her gifts all set for the morning. Stockings for all, and goodies inside. No coal this year, unless her little brothers pulled something funny during the play that night.

"You have kids, Coach Ketch?" She used his nickname from when she was in school and he was a history teacher there.

He shook his head. "Didn't quite get the chance to have my own. But my athletes are like my sons now. And my students like my daughters." He smiled at her.

"I came by to collect Greta and Tabby. She'll need a bottle and a change before we come back later for mass. Then the lighting." Coach Hart nodded toward the group assembled at the front of the parish hall.

"Oh," Gretchen answered. Something in her deflated. Hope, maybe, that they were bringing some word about Theo. That he was looking for her. Sort of like Miss Fern had been looking for him. It sure seemed like the two men had a little extra time on their hands as the women scrambled around town tying Christmas together. *Men.* Gretchen smirked inwardly.

"I gotta head out," Coach Ketchum murmured. "I promised Fern and Stedman I'd bring a few tables and chairs over from the high school. Gotta pick him up from the house there on Pine Tree and head over."

"You'd better hurry," Gretchen said, imagining Liesel still there with Miss Fern. Her pretty red nails and done-up hair and Christmas sweater on display and for what? For who?

Could it be... for *him*? Mark Ketchum?

No, Gretchen realized flatly. Opposites to that degree would probably *never* attract.

CHAPTER 14—LIESEL

Liesel needn't have worried if Fern had held onto that baby quilt from so, *so* long ago. Of course, she had. It wasn't even stowed away, either. It was laid out neatly on the edge of her guest room bed, a pretty homage to her earliest days in Hickory Grove. Her very first friend, too. A friend she wouldn't quite connect with until years later. Indeed, Liesel and Fern were still working on that connection now.

"I'll bring it back," Liesel told Fern, admiring the red and white fabric she'd tended so carefully with her mother. She ran a hand over a block, the half-square triangles tugging her sorely to the past. Liesel hadn't made another shoo-fly quilt ever since this one. She'd never make another, either. Too hard to revisit the memory now, now that her mother was gone.

Fern grabbed Liesel's hand. "I don't have children, Liesel," she said, stating the obvious.

Liesel blinked. "Neither do I."

They laughed together, softly, then Liesel thanked Fern. She didn't know she wanted the quilt back.

Until that very day.

Stedman called up the stairs to his wife. He'd finished his chore: half a cord of chopped and split wood for the bonfire. Liesel thanked Fern and took her leave.

She had to get dressed and ready for mass and the lighting and, somehow, come up with dinner plans. Maybe the priest would take her in? Or Greta and Luke? Liesel could cook for them at the Inn to keep things convenient. She could just kick herself for not having the forethought to make some sort of arrangement.

Then it dawned on her: the Hickory Grove Community Christmas Dinner.

It was still on for the very next evening. She'd helped coordinate and plan for it. No, she hadn't intended to go, of course, but that wouldn't mean the Charitable Committee wouldn't appreciate her appearance.

That was it. Liesel would attend the children's mass then head to the tree lighting and call it a night. And the next day, instead of barreling into the family celebrations of her nephew, like a female version of Scrooge, she'd have her own engagement. Something near and dear to her heart and so full of Christmas spirit that she'd have her fill and then some. She could move on to her new project and to the new season and do just fine. She'd made it through another lonesome year. She could make it through another one after that. And then another, until one day—maybe not until she was seventy or eighty—but *one* day Liesel would find her one and true vocation. The thing she was meant for.

But somewhere deep down inside, Liesel knew that it wasn't some*thing* she was meant for. It was some*one*. And by the time she found him, she wondered if she'd wasted all those years on silly deals with herself. Silly, useless projects. Like giving away the last quilt her mother ever made. Or planning an entire Christmas vacation to Michigan only to skip it all together.

Or, the notion that not only was she going to *vacation* to Michigan. She was going to stay there, too.

Maybe, Liesel thought, as she drove the slick, white-trimmed streets up and down slippery Hickory Grove hills, *maybe* she'd still find herself in Michigan. Soon. And for *good*.

THE CHILDREN'S mass was as precious as could be. Little Briar, Maggie's youngest, making a fine—if premature—Mary. And Tabby, the little cherub, as Baby Jesus. It was too much to take, and Liesel wished she'd never planned to leave town on such a special day.

"Okay," Greta said to Luke, scooping Tabby from him and rocking her gently as others made their ways from the parish hall. "You go ahead and get the turkey carved. Take Mark. I'll be a little behind. I want to touch base with Gretchen, first."

Luke bent and kissed his wife and daughter then turned to Liesel. "See you soon!" He spun and left, and Liesel realized that maybe, after all, she *did* get an invitation to the Hart Family Christmas. She didn't even have to ask.

Still, it'd be rude to presume. "See me soon?" she reverberated to Greta.

Greta cocked her head. "Well, you're coming over for supper, first, right?"

Liesel watched Luke head to the doors. She blinked and looked back at Greta. "Oh, that is very kind of you, sweet-heart. But—don't you need to ride together?"

"Oh, no, we came separately," Greta answered. "I drove

alone with Tabby. Mark and Luke came together. *Late.*" Greta's eyes widened as if embarrassed. "They were finishing things up for the tree lighting, you see."

"Mark?" Liesel still couldn't quite come to terms with how much Mark Ketchum was around of late. Sure, she saw him every week at mass. And in the past few years, he'd become a regular at the Hickory Grove Community Christmas. But his passion was football and history. And Liesel's was, well... well, she was still trying to figure it out. Though they found themselves running in the same circles, so to speak, they had nothing much to do with one another.

Other than the one thing that bugged Liesel to no end.

The quilt.

Her mother's last quilt. Mark Ketchum *technically* owned it.

There was just one way around that problem. Liesel would have to make another. And maybe, what with the Michigan trip over for now, maybe Liesel had an opportunity to do just that.

And maybe she had someone to help this time around, too.

Greta lifted her voice across the room to where Maggie Devereux stood with her family, including, it would now appear, Theo Linden. "You all coming over?"

Liesel blinked. She figured Greta and Luke would invite Gretchen, sure. Gretchen might even be on duty at the Inn that night. However, for the whole family to come over? It'd be pure chaos. What about the guests at the Inn?

She swallowed, reconsidering her plan to accept the invitation and swing by the market to pick up an extra jug of eggnog and some fresh vegetables to chop up for Greta.

"Be there with bells on!" Maggie hollered back, tickling

her little Briar into submission as the rest of the family cooed over the little girl's all-star performance.

Gretchen appeared at Greta's side and Tabby curled her little fist around Gretchen's finger. Her swaddling clothes— that familiar shoo-fly pattern splayed around the child like flower petals, turned Liesel's heart to mush.

Greta indicated the old blanket. "I tried to untangle her from it after the play, but she cried and cried. Seems the only way to keep her content is to leave it be. I'll get this back to you right away, though, Aunt Liesel."

Aunt Liesel shook her head. "Oh, no." She glanced up toward the pews, where Fern still lingered. Their conversation fresh in her mind. "That quilt is in want of a new owner. It's Tabby's now."

Greta beamed. "Are you sure?"

"I'm sure."

Tabby cooed and gaggled and Liesel buzzed inwardly. As though her mother had predicted this all so many years ago, the blanket had made its rounds. And, with any luck, it'd continue on its journey, in that winding way that quilts often do.

"You're coming with us, right Miss Liesel?" Gretchen interjected.

Liesel shook her head. "I have to help Fern."

"Help Fern do *what*? She'll be with us!" Greta cried. "Luke was supposed to tell you. We're hosting half the town at the Inn. It'll be crazy. It'll be *great*. You've got to come."

Furrowing her brow, Liesel considered the alternative: sit at home for a couple of hours until it was time for the lighting? Alone?

"I have a project. A new quilt I need to work on," she said at last, realizing that's *exactly* what she'd do.

"A new quilt?" Gretchen's interest clearly piqued. "That's just perfect! I'd love to see it."

"I haven't started yet," Liesel confessed, her cheeks flushing. "And anyway, it's hard to bring around an active project."

"I could help you plan it. I hear that a lot of planning goes into quilt-making." Gretchen wasn't going to take no for an answer.

Theo came up behind her. "Come on, Miss Liesel. Mark Ketchum will be there."

Liesel's cheeks grew redder, and she took a step back. "So?" She came across as cutting and defensive, but she couldn't help it. What was it all of a sudden with Mark Ketchum?

"We can talk quilts tomorrow maybe. Or the next day when it's less busy," Liesel assured Gretchen.

Becky Linden and Fern Gale and their church dates appeared from the parish hall. "She's coming all right," Fern said. "Liesel, you work too hard not to enjoy a little merry-making, I'll say."

"Merry-making?" Liesel couldn't help but allow a grin to curl across her face.

"That's right," Maggie chimed in, a spent and adorable Briar resting her head on her mama's shoulder. "Christmastime merry-making. Drinks and food and great company. And then? The annual Christmas tree lighting at Hickory Grove's own *Christmas House*."

"Come on, Liesel." Becky elbowed her. "You're in town. What else do you have planned for the holiday anyway?"

"Tomorrow night's supper. The charitable supper."

"That's tomorrow," Fern replied, her tone sharp. "Tonight, you can *relax*."

"Relax *and* talk shop with Gretchen. I'm telling you,

Liesel," Maggie went on, rubbing Briar's back, "if you don't help this girl get a little experience with quilting, she's liable to open a crafting shop and not know a *lick* about it."

"There's more to crafting than just quilting," Liesel pointed out. But they were now all walking to the cars, her agreement implied as she sidled up to Gretchen. "You know that, right?"

Gretchen nodded urgently. "Quilting is my main goal. I like sewing well enough. But I'm no seamstress or tailor or garment maker. And as for crocheting and knitting—it's not big enough. I need a *real* project. Something to get the feel for what fabric-shoppers and needle-buyers *do*."

"And quilting is a real project, eh?" Liesel asked as she waved to Maggie and the others and Theo dawdled sweetly behind Gretchen.

Liesel glanced up at Little Flock parish as she stood near her car. The white steeple bled into the white-dusted trees in the landscape around it, as if the church was *one* with the town, which, really, it was.

Liesel glanced down at her own outfit—a white sweater dress over fleece-lined leggings, tucked down into snuggly brown, knee-high winter boots. Maybe she, too, was one with the town.

Or at least, one with her *community*.

Of course, quilting was a real project. And it would teach Gretchen everything she needed to learn.

Just as it had Liesel.

STEP 6: BIND THE LAYERS

"There are two ways to add binding. The right way and the lazy way. Turns out, however, that the lazy way will give your quilt added strength."

Liesel was surprised by this. Typically, the opposite was true. The harder way was the better way.

"The lazy way, we use the extra backing, flipping it over like so." She showed Liesel what she meant. "The other way, we cut new binding and sew it on. Your choice, Liesel."

Liesel's eyebrows shot up. Nothing had been her choice yet. Not with this project. "The lazy way, then. If it makes the quilt stronger, why would anyone do it the other way?"

"Depends on the quilter. Remember, quilters are artists. Maybe there's a fabric conflict, and you don't want the backing material to be seen along your top. Maybe you were always taught to add binding separately."

"I told the ladies at church they could use this quilt for the Baby Jesus's swaddling clothes. Is that all right?" Liesel knew better than to do something like that without first asking her mother. She'd been nervous to bring up the matter and so kept her eyes downcast on the table.

"You want to give your quilt to Little Flock, then? For use in their Nativity play each year?"

Liesel shrugged.

"Or you want to give the quilt to little Fern?" her mother added.

She hadn't thought that far ahead. All she'd thought about was the Boy Child's swaddling clothes.

"I'm not sure. The church could probably use it. But what about Fern? What if she wants to keep it?"

"Good point," her mother answered. "We can always make blankets for the church. It could become a tradition, even. Fern might like to have the quilt. Just wait and see. Sometimes, you don't know a quilt's destiny until it presents itself."

Liesel gave a short nod, and off they went, binding the three layers together into what her mother called a sandwich, which Liesel felt was distinctly un-quilting-like language.

After a day, they'd finished the binding, and Liesel was worn out on quilting.

They admired the project together, looking for errors—there were plenty—and studying the blocks.

"It's beautiful," Liesel decided, folding her arms over her chest and grinning from ear to ear.

"You've done a great job, Liesel."

"Should we wrap it? Like in brown paper?"

"And tie it up with strings?" her mother asked, laughing. "Well, we aren't done yet."

"Not done?" Liesel might faint. "What else is there to do?"

"Oh, my darlin' child, the most important part! This isn't even a quilt yet."

CHAPTER 15—GRETCHEN

They were back at the Inn, and the dining room was packed, the parlor was packed, the kitchen was packed - with sweater-wearing guests, each holding a plate of food up to their chins as they laughed and swapped stories.

Gretchen's heart was bursting at the seams with contentedness. In the past two years, she'd endured her fair share of hardship. Her parents' divorce. Almost a week of vagrancy where she'd been right there, upstairs sharing a twin bed with Briar while her mother and brothers slept next door, fitful and fearful and distracted. That was a ways before Greta and Luke got together and took on the Hickory Grove Inn. Before they hired Gretchen. Before this Christmas Eve.

Now here they *all* were—Maggie with Rhett and the three younger kids. Gretchen's mama was happy as could be, living, loving, and doing hair out of her farmhouse kitchen like a regular southern-style stay-at-home mama.

Miss Fern and Stedman were re-settled in the Christmas House, which had officially become the Hickory Grove

Museum. They worked it together. They did almost *everything* together. Happy and *connected*.

Miss Greta and Luke and little sweet Tabby in her swaddling quilt had found success running old Mamaw Hart's bed and breakfast and living in her home, the innkeeper's house.

Miss Becky and Mr. Durbin married and shared his house in town. During the days, he had his law practice and she her bookshop, The Schoolhouse. Theo was now just a year out of graduating. A year away from coming back home. Or close to it, at least.

And here she was, Gretchen. With Theo now. *Again*. Maybe forever? And with her dream within grasp. That was, so long as she could get Miss Liesel alone and pitch the idea she had bubbling in her chest ever since she realized she *was* staying in Hickory Grove. And she *was* making something of her barn. And she *was* doing everything she set out to do, all she needed now was a *guide*. And Liesel was *it*!

Somebody in the parlor clinked their glass with a knife, the shrill bell effect drawing the friends and bed-and-breakfast guests together in a thick crowd.

It was Coach Hart, calling the crowd in to explain dessert.

"We've got four dishes, and each one was handmade by a Hickory woman."

The attendants laughed good-naturedly.

"Well, they were. And if I've remembered right, Maggie made the pecan pie. Fern the double chocolate chip cookies. Becky the bread pudding. And Greta the Christmas Crack, a Hart Family favorite, I might add. Dig in, everyone. Go on. Then we'll all leave for the lighting within half an hour. Can't be late to that."

As he lowered his glass of eggnog and the crowd began

to disperse back toward the kitchen buffet, the front door creaked open, the bells above it clanging jingle jangle to life.

"Speaking of late," Theo whispered to Gretchen, and her gaze flew to the door.

Coach Ketchum ambled in, a nervous wince to his face as he drew the attention of those lingering around the edge of the foyer.

Gretchen smiled at him and took a step his way. "Coach Ketchum, glad you could make it."

"Sorry I'm late. I—" he held up a casserole dish and peeled back one corner to reveal the burnt crust of something that looked vaguely like meatloaf. Then he dipped back through the front door and tugged in two oversized paper bags, corner market issue.

"No, no. Lots of us are still working on supper."

Coach Ketchum gave a nod to Gretchen. "Theo, hi there. How's school? Your mama was telling me just one year left. That right?"

"Yessir," Theo answered. Though raised in an area where few youth ever used *sir* or *madam*, Theo had caught on quickly enough when he was in town.

"You know I intended to make my way to law school one day, too," the older man revealed. As he said this, something cracked open in the façade of a teacher who Gretchen thought she had pegged. A small-town high school teacher by day. Football coach by night. Misspent youth being what it was, Gretchen, somewhere deep down, had always just figured him for a would-be athlete type. Someone who yearned for the good old days of locker-room hijinks and championship weekends.

"Law school?" Gretchen asked, her stare sliding to Theo. "Just like you." When she looked back at the middle-aged teacher, she thought she saw him as Mark for a fleeting second. Rather than Coach or Coach Ketchum or Mr. Ketchum. She saw, well... *Theo* in him. And she wondered if that isn't what could become of her boyfriend, too. A local teacher who coached to make ends meet or relive his glory days or *whatever*. But, then, Theo was no jock, and that had been a point of interest for Gretchen. A difference about him. Something that set him distinctly outside of Hickory Grove and in the greater world. Something that Gretchen *liked* about Theo.

"That's right. I took the LSAT. Got a decent score, but by then I'd started student teaching, and—I just couldn't see myself ever doing anything else."

"You felt stuck?" Gretchen asked, dancing dangerously close to a personal line she had no right to cross. She wasn't even asking for herself at this point, though. She was asking for Liesel. Another person who Gretchen considered to be, well, *stuck*.

"Not at'all," Coach answered earnestly, jauntily, even. "I fell in love."

Gretchen couldn't help but let her eyes bulge. She'd known Coach Ketchum was married once, but it wasn't something he spoke of. She'd died, that wife. And it had left its mark. Figuring the wife was what he meant, she nodded respectfully and murmured an apology.

"No, I mean with teaching. I worked at a Catholic School for years, you know. Loved it there. St. Agatha's up north. I learned a lot about snow and a lot about God in those days. Then I met my wife, we moved here, and I took up locally. And that was just fine, too."

Surprised that his love had more to do with his career than the woman he'd married, something tightened in Gretchen's chest, like a cinch. Discomfort.

"I know what that's like," Theo cut into the conversation

and wrapped his arm around Gretchen's waist. She flushed and frowned at him. He smiled at her. "Realizing that as humans, we make plans, but then along comes God, turning them into paper airplanes on a breezy day."

The room shrunk in on them, but Gretchen realized Coach Ketchum had left, and gone, too, were those other guests who'd been chatting between the foyer and the parlor. It was just Theo and she there, now. And his eyes were on her, intense and unmoving.

"Your plans are changing now, too?" she asked him, confused. Was he or *wasn't* he going to Louisville? What? Was this all a *game* to Theo? Was Gretchen stupid to think they'd ever be anything other than a couple playing house?

"No," he answered, his stare narrowing tighter on her, as he released his arm from her waist and moved both hands. Their hands found each other. "I'm going to Louisville. I wasn't, before. When you ended things, I applied to the UofA, ASU, New Mexico—anywhere that wasn't here. But then I did a lot of thinking and I remembered what you said."

"What did I say?"

"You said you wanted to get of town, but not for good. That you'd stay here and open a business, and now look at you, Gretchen."

"What?" She wished she *could* look at herself. She'd scarcely had time to put on makeup before Mass. Her reunion with Theo was unexpected, and her attention was split between that and finding Liesel and pinning her down before she could run off to Michigan without that quilting lesson.

"You're opening a business," he said.

At that, Gretchen frowned deep. "I mean," she started, blinking, "I *want* to, but that doesn't mean all that much."

"But—"

"Theo. Gretchen."

Liesel's voice startled them both, but Gretchen saw Theo turn slightly pale. He cleared his throat and hooked a thumb at Miss Liesel. "I'll um..." his eyes darted from Liesel to Gretchen twice, settling at last on Gretchen, whom he pecked on the cheek. "I'll go get us each a slice of pie. Pumpkin, right?"

He knew her well. Her lips pricked into a smile and she nodded at him.

"I have an idea," Liesel said to Gretchen when they were alone together.

CHAPTER 16—LIESEL

I t was a wild idea. But it was a good one. What's more?
It'd force Liesel to have roots somewhere. Roots of her
own. Roots she could share with another soul on this
earth, too.

She had the money. Her mother's. She had the time.
Plenty.

She just needed the inspiration.

But it was a big offer, and it was an offer she didn't care
to enter lightly into. So, instead of first approaching
Gretchen, she went to Maggie, tugging her away from Rhett
and into the hall at the Inn, a private conversation among
adults concerning another, emerging adult.

With Maggie's blessing, Liesel next went to Theo. She
could see plain as day the boy's plan, and if this might inter-
fere, then she'd drop it.

He swore up and down that it wouldn't, though. And so,
after talking to him and running some figures through her
head—Liesel knew her own finances well—she stole a
moment alone to compose her thoughts. She'd missed

Luke's dessert spiel and had precious little time before they'd set off for the lighting.

She'd been in the hall that stretched from the foyer to the little closet beyond the front desk, and so when she overheard Theo start to reveal her inquiry, she darted out as fast as Santa flew down chimneys.

"Idea?" Gretchen asked, her cheeks pink, though whether from the weather, or Theo, or even Liesel, it was hard to tell.

"Your crafting store idea. I want to help you."

"You'll teach me to quilt, then?" Gretchen asked, her eyes sparkling.

"I'll teach you, yes. But also, I'll invest. I'll—I'll help you finish the barn and convert it however you see fit. Is that where you'd like to have the shop?"

Gretchen was processing the offer, that much was clear. Her eyebrows fell low down to her eyes, her mouth twitched. "Invest... you mean, like, you'll help me get started?"

"In every way I can, yes," Liesel confirmed, smiling. "From the ground up. We'll order inventory. Decorate together. I'll help you host your first quilting class, too."

"Oh, Miss Liesel, but... but Michigan? And... Little Flock and everything else you do. What about Tabby? And Luke and Greta? Your time and money are surely better spent on them."

"It's an investment, not just a gift. We'll do this *together*, Gretchen. Anyway, I was looking for a new project to sink my needles into." She winked at Gretchen and pulled the slender girl in for a tight hug.

"We can call it L&G Crafts and More."

"I think," Liesel replied, "if you don't mind, I have a better name."

Before she could divulge it, however, they were interrupted.

"Liesel?"

She whipped around to find Mark Ketchum standing there. His Christmas sweater a deep burgundy wool thing. His slacks, pressed to within an inch of their starch-stricken life, a harsh line dragging past each of his knees. He looked itchy. And nervous. And out of sorts. And... adorable.

Liesel tugged discreetly at the neck of her own sweater. "Mark, hi." She flicked a glance to Gretchen. "Were you looking for... Theo? Or Luke?"

He shook his head and licked his lips. "Um." Then, he cleared his throat before dropping his voice. "No. I'm looking for you."

Liesel reddened as Gretchen excused herself, slipping into the rest of the party like a partridge in a pear tree. Liesel watched her go, desperately hoping she'd turn around and drag Liesel away with her.

No such luck.

"Sorry if I'm bothering you?" It was more a question than an apology.

Liesel felt compelled to offer him assurance. "Oh, of course not." It had been ages since she'd chatted with Mark. Truly chatted. In fact, the last time she could remember was years back, when her mother was still alive, at that Community Christmas Dinner.

Her gaze fell to his hand from which a bag hung. Brown paper. A red piece of yarn was tied neatly, in a small bow around the handles.

He lifted the bag. "Merry Christmas," he said. "I've been meaning to get this to you for a while now."

Her brows fell in, but a smile played on her mouth. "A while, huh? What is it?"

Something deep inside told Liesel he hadn't necessarily intended to exchange gifts with her.

"It's yours," he said. "And it's time it found its way back."

He passed her the bag, and their fingertips brushed.

Liesel didn't have to open it to know what was inside. She didn't even have to peek. She handed it back. "No, it's *yours*," she said, her stare intent on him. His on her, too.

Mark cocked his head. "How do you know what it is?"

Liesel closed her eyes for a moment, pressed her hand to her head then looked at him again. "I made that quilt for a *reason*. And it was meant for you, Mark. Still is." Inside, she wondered, though, if this wasn't her quilt's special journey. Its way back to her. Her face froze as she studied the bag in her own hand now. She lifted it back towards him. "Please."

"Well," Mark answered, accepting the bag and dropping his chin, "maybe we can share it? Tonight, at the tree lighting? I'm taking my truck over, and I could use a good blanket to sit on."

STEP 7—FINISH THE QUILT

"**L**et me get this straight," Liesel said to her mother as she set up the sewing machine, "we've patched nine blocks together, added batting and backing, and we haven't made a quilt yet?"

"Well, we've been quilting, yes. We've been making a quilt, that is," her mother replied, lining up two markers—one in front of each of them.

"We've been quilting this whole time, but we don't have a quilt yet?"

"No, Liesel," her mother answered. "It's not a quilt until you quilt the quilt. Until then, it's a blanket." She laughed, that warm, buttery laugh, soft and sweet and low. Liesel couldn't well be mad at the woman now. They'd come this far.

Still, she couldn't imagine spending another day on the project. "Let's just leave it as a blanket," Liesel suggested.

Her mother frowned and dismissed the notion without hesitation. "Where's the fun? Where's the artistry?"

"The magic," Liesel whispered.

Her mother's face pulled serious, and she nodded. "Now, you get it."

It took them another few days to finish the final sewing, pretty patterns for Liesel to play with, before it was time for the quilt to head out on its journey. A journey that Liesel couldn't well predict. Who knew what would become of Little Fern? Or Liesel's mother, or Liesel even, for that matter? Or Little Flock?

Liesel and her mother laid the finished quilt across the kitchen table. It had been a while since the Hart family had enjoyed supper there together, and the boys were starting to get cranky about it.

But now, looking at the nine blocks—three rows stacked neatly with that precious, simple shoo-fly pattern—Liesel didn't much care what the boys were cranky about. She was proud. Prouder than she'd ever been in her life. Proud of herself and, strangely, proud of her mother. Seeing the woman through this light—as an intimate teacher, a leader, and a mentor... but also as an artist... it was moving. So moving, indeed, that Liesel felt a bit emotional to give the thing away at all.

"Maybe we should keep it."

Her mother smoothed her hand down the center of the quilt then looked at Liesel. "You'll make more."

"It's my first one," Liesel argued.

"True," her mother answered. Then she smiled. "It's your decision."

"When can I start on the next one?" Liesel asked.

Her mother laughed. "I thought you were burnt out?"

Liesel shrugged. "I'm addicted, I think."

"You can start as soon as you'd like. Though, you'll need more fabric, and to get more fabric, you'll need money."

Sighing, Liesel stared hard at the quilt. The first she'd ever made. With her mother's help, but still...

"I'll give this one to Fern. They need it for the Nativity anyway. And as for fabric, well, I'll... I'll take on odd jobs."

"I can pay you to turn beds. Same as I pay the other housekeepers." Her mother had offered Liesel this part-time job over and again, although it never sat quite right with her. Then again, previously, Liesel hadn't cared to make any money. Money, to her, was simply for covering the necessities.

Now, it would appear, fabric had become a necessity. "I'll turn beds and do whatever I need to," Liesel answered determinedly.

"Remember how I told you that some ladies will send their quilts out for binding and even the final sewing?"

"Yes." Liesel waited with bated breath for her mother's next great idea.

"Do you know ol' Miss Devereux, the seamstress?"

"Of course. She's running the Nativity."

"She used to do that. She used to take in other ladies' quilts and finish them. Up there in that barn next to her house on the edge of town. She called the place The Quilting House."

Liesel's eyes grew wide. "The Quilting House. Just like our house, here!"

"That's the last rule of quilting, Liesel," her mother said. Her tone was serious and deep and her eyes hard on her daughter. She grabbed both of Liesel's hands. "We might be artists. And there might be magic. But the fact is, Liesel, we don't create these quilts."

Confused as ever, Liesel gave her mother a skeptical look. "We don't?"

Her mother shook her head. "Only God creates. The rest of us? We're just kicking around great ideas, inspired by our mothers and our mothers' mothers and all the other great women we know. Each in our own Quilting House. Each with our own patterns, stitched together like patchwork." She smiled and curled her finger beneath Liesel's chin. "Just like you and me."

CHAPTER 17—GRETCHEN

As soon as they arrived at Miss Fern's house on Pine Tree Lane, Gretchen felt magic in the air. She always did, at every tree lighting every year, but she'd been worried about this one. Having it on Christmas Eve, as opposed to weeks earlier, as was tradition, had felt *off*. Rushed. Wrong, even. Why Miss Fern made the change was beyond Gretchen's knowledge. Beyond anyone's it seemed. Her mother didn't know. Rhett didn't. Neither did Becky or Liesel. All they knew was that they'd be rushing around all day until that very night.

And still, despite the rushing and the business of the day, magic hung in that twilit sky above Hickory Grove, the North star shining particularly bright, Gretchen noticed, despite the matching glow of the great big Christmas tree, anchored centrally on the front yard and peopled on all sides. The merriness and cheer were palpable as people sang Christmas carols and bubbled over.

Some folks stood near a roaring bonfire off to the side. Some lingered near the hot cocoa station, manned by Gretchen's two little brothers, impossibly. She grinned.

Then others backed their trucks onto the edge of the grass near the street. Too far to be close enough to partake in the sweets and carols, but close enough to get a piece of the Christmas action—to see the lights but to mind their own.

Gretchen and Theo were the latter. They parked his truck, and he unfolded a thick flannel blanket, spreading it on his tailgate.

"I'm going to get us a couple of cups of cocoa," she told him. "Want to come?"

Theo fumbled in his reply. Maybe his lips were numb from the cold. Or he was tired. She sure was, after all. "Um, oh. Right. Um. Just—yeah, go ahead. Or, wait. I'll come, too."

"Okay," she smirked and laughed to herself but took his arm. He walked her up the drive, freshly shoveled and coated in rock salt for just this occasion. Their breath came out in frosty pillows on the air, and Gretchen peered hard through the crowd to spot her mother or Miss Liesel. Anyone, really. Anyone to smile and nod to.

First, they happened upon Theo's mom and Zack Durbin. Instead of a greeting, Becky sort of hissed through the night to her son, "Well?"

Theo froze up all over again and shook his mom off, apologizing to Gretchen for her being *weird*, although Gretchen was entirely too preoccupied with spotting Miss Fern and Stedman, greeting people as they entered the hot cocoa line.

"How's it going, *Theo*?" Fern asked pointedly. Gretchen glanced at him, and again he sort of shook his head and shrugged, short-circuiting.

Gretchen whispered, "What's going on?"

"Nothing," he answered. "Just, *nothing*."

They grabbed their drinks and made their way back toward the truck, where she looked forward to cuddling and sipping and cuddling some more. But then she spied Miss Liesel.

"Oh, shoot," she murmured beneath her breath.

"What is it?" Theo slowed for her, and together they looked on as, miracle of miracles, Liesel held the arm of none other than Coach Ketchum as they walked up the drive toward the cocoa station.

Gretchen couldn't contain the overweening smile that filled her face. "Miss Liesel," she said, all but giggling. "Coach Ketchum. Merry Christmas."

"Merry Christmas," the two answered in tandem, effectively solidifying their status as a couple on a *date*.

"We'll have to talk soon, right?" Gretchen added when they slowed in passing. "About the quilting investment. The business name?" She was trying to stall the woman to further assess them but also jog her memory about where they'd left off.

"Yes," Liesel answered. "We're partners now. We'll have to meet up at ol' Marguerite Devereux's shop. You know where it is. I think she was your great aunt, after all." Liesel winked at a befuddled Gretchen, and off she went, on the arm of a dashing local man. Someone who maybe, just maybe, Liesel had something in common with after all. Even if it was just a *thread*.

By the time Gretchen and Theo made it back to his truck, her fingers and toes had grown numb, but blood was coursing through her body, warming her chest and limbs well enough that she managed to hop onto the tailgate and nest herself into Theo.

"Do you know why they moved the tree lighting to tonight?" Theo asked her as "O Come All Ye Faithful" drifted from the caroling crowd. They'd start any moment now. Fern would count down, and there would be a cheer and *flash*, the star at the top of the Christmas tree would come to light. Couples would kiss. Children would squeal— the first hint of what was in store in their stockings later that night.

"No. No one knows," Gretchen answered, sipping her drink carefully so as not to burn her tongue. She'd hate to have a burned tongue on Christmas Eve. With Theo there. She twisted to look at him, but he was staring off, his question irrelevant or random. She frowned and leaned away. He glanced down at her. "Theo? Do *you* know why Fern moved it to tonight?"

He drew his finger to his lips, quieting her as the song pulled to a low murmur and Fern began her countdown.

She got to one, and the star lit up, brilliant against the white blanketed earth and huddled masses. It almost appeared as though half the crowd sort of turned and looked toward the street, at Gretchen, even. But that couldn't be.

Theo popped off the tailgate, despite the fact they'd only just gotten comfortable.

About to ask if he was okay or where he was going, Gretchen was silenced by a mounting pressure—the air, warmer for some reason and suffocating, almost. Theo grabbed her hands and pulled her off the tailgate, too. And then they were standing together, there, at the edge of Fern's tree lighting, right by his tailgate, where that heavy flannel blanket draped so comfortably. Were there pillows in the back of the truck? Was Gretchen seeing things?

Faces appeared in the near-distance behind Theo. All familiar. Each aglow with a single white candle stick floating beneath it, like a Christmas choir out for Christmas carols and then—

Theo lowered to the ground. One knee. Deep, *deep* in the snow, almost like he was sinking, but he wasn't. He was twisting away to retrieve something from his coat pocket.

A gold box. As if in slow motion, Gretchen saw it all— she saw him remove a second box within—this one white velvet. And then he returned his attention to Gretchen and lifted the white box, opening its lid. Inside, a glimmering solitaire diamond protruded from a dark gold ring. Unconventional for the modern age, but familiar. Beautiful and familiar and antique.

"Gretchen Engel," Theo whispered, nearly a dozen candles burning in the background, "will you marry me?"

EPILOGUE

It was Liesel's grandmother's wedding ring which Theo had used to propose. That accounted for the familiarity. Found amongst the family heirlooms in one of the boxes. The bands they exchanged at their intimate wedding ceremony a year later were also heirloom pieces—Theo's grandparents', Grandbern and Memaw Linden. Memaw was still alive but more than happy to contribute her band. What she hoped, she'd said, was that Theo and Gretchen would one day have a son or daughter with whom to share her engagement ring. That was the deal in Hickory Grove, after all. Things just floated down, down, down the family line and out into the roots of the town, some way, somehow.

The ceremony took place at the farm, the place she'd be moving away from now that she and Theo were married. He'd been accepted into law school at Louisville, as he planned. They would stay on in the barn until Rhett and Theo finished building a house for them—a real one—on the farm but an acre off, to provide for some privacy for the newlyweds.

Until then, though, they'd have the barn.

Or, as Liesel and Gretchen had since named it: The Quilting House.

In the six months since Liesel first posited her idea of investing in Gretchen's business, they'd built a solid foundation, initially with Liesel walking Gretchen through her first quilt (a shoo-fly block pattern, or, as Gretchen chose to call it, the hole in the barn door). After that first quilt, which took over a month to finish, what with Gretchen's two jobs, she found that she could give her notice at Malley's. This was easier said than done, and Gretchen often found herself enjoying a milkshake and a hamburger there some late afternoons, just for old time's sake.

As for Liesel, she'd set about researching what a small-town craft store could do for a community. Turned out, it was more than just selling good yarn and fine thread. They'd have classes. Regular classes they'd hold open to the community. Some free. Some paid. It'd all balance out. And with Mark Ketchum and Hickory Grove Unified providing his classroom as a designated space, it worked out quite well.

Over those months, Mark and Liesel spent more time together, too. Mainly when Gretchen was working at the Inn or enjoying dates with Theo, Liesel and Mark would take day trips here and there. It was funny, their commonalities. They had more than they'd ever have guessed.

Of course, that quilt got some good use. Between fish frys and tailgate parties and simple, quiet nights together under the stars, Liesel realized that everything her mother had ever taught her, turned out to be right.

The comfort in that was almost enough to allow Liesel to rest easy on the matter of her own origins.

Almost.

"Congratulations," Liesel said to Gretchen and Theo as they made their way over to where she sat with Mark, at a back table, out of the way and close to the road, where Mark's truck sat, packed and waiting.

"Thank you," Gretchen gushed. "Thank you for *everything* you've done, Liesel. I mean it." Theo gave Liesel a peck on the cheek and echoed his new bride's sentiments.

Once they'd left, Liesel squeezed Mark's hand. He dipped his chin toward her. "You're sure you want to do this?"

She nodded. "Only reason I'd have had a wedding would have been for my mom. But since she's up there now," Liesel pointed to the sky, "I reckon she'll get to come along for the ride anyway."

Liesel and Mark were eloping. To a beautiful town off the shores of Lake Huron. A place Liesel had been content to give up on but still harbored curiosities about. Especially when she came to learn that there was a little Catholic school *there*. A place where young mothers used to stay until they had their babies. The place where Liesel Hart was born. Probably where she'd been wrapped in her very first quilt, too.

A place called *Heirloom Island*.

If you enjoyed this story, be sure to order *The Boardwalk House, An Heirloom Island Novel* to see where Liesel and Mark's adventure takes them.

Join Elizabeth Bromke's reader club today at
elizabethbromke.com.

Looking for a different read? Check out the bestselling series, *Birch Harbor*.

ALSO BY ELIZABETH BROMKE

Birch Harbor:

House on the Harbor

Lighthouse on the Lake

Fireflies in the Field

Cottage by the Creek

Bells on the Bay

Gull's Landing:

The Summer Society, a USA Today Bestseller

The Garden Guild

The Country Club

Harbor Hills:

The House on Apple Hill Lane

The House with the Blue Front Door

The House Around the Corner

The House that Christmas Made

The Hickory Grove Series

ACKNOWLEDGMENTS

What a treat to return to Hickory Grove, Indiana! And along for the ride came some of my dear old friends, including Lisa Lee, my editor, and Tandy O., my proofreader. Thank you both, ladies, for polishing this story up.

My advanced reader team is a special group. Without you, a critical final step of my process would be missing. Thank you for being my cheerleaders!

My friends, especially Mel, Rachael, Gigi, Pam, Cindy, Jan, Lee, Kay, and Charity—thank you for your support in our little corner of the world! Also, to my friends Meagan, Shannon, Erin, and Kara (sisters, in fact) who unwittingly star in each of my books about female friendship. Your influence is precious to me.

Always my family: my parents, brother, sisters, grand-folks, aunts, uncles, cousins, in-laws... thank you for giving me the tight-knit world of Hickory Grove! My Aunt Margot, Aunt Jody, and Grandpa E. in heaven: I miss you all and think of you often. Love you.

Ed and Eddie, and Winnie, too! I love you so much!!!

ABOUT THE AUTHOR

After graduating from the University of Arizona, Elizabeth Bromke became an English teacher. You can still find her in a classroom today, behind a stack of essays and a leaning tower of classic novels.

When she's not teaching, Elizabeth writes women's fiction and contemporary romance. For fun, she enjoys jigsaw puzzles, crosswords, and—of course—reading.

Elizabeth lives in the northern mountains of Arizona with her husband, son, and their sweet dog Winnie.

Learn more about the author by visiting her website at elizabethbromke.com.